AL MORENO
RIFT
RESOLVER

AND THE
CRYSTAL OF
GOSIA

Mason J. Schneider

Note: This is a work of fiction. All the
characters and events portrayed in this
book are fictitious, and any resemblance
to real people or events is purely
coincidental.

Al Moreno: Rift Resolver And the Crystal
of Gosia

Cover art by MiblArt

www.riftresolver.com

ISBN: 978-1-0934-8182-2

Other Works
By Mason J. Schneider

Al Moreno Rift Resolver Series:

The Solution For Thear – Book Two

The Wizard of the Night Series:

Wizarded Away – Book One

Contents

Praise for Al Moreno Rift Resolver and a Word of Warning to Hardcore Science Fiction Fans:

"A breezy, campy space opera that delivers a close encounter of the retro-pulp kind."

- Kirkus Reviews

Now, it should be noted that this is a tale more closely aligned with the pulp-fiction days of old. Although it is set in the future and references advanced technology, the actual science behind some of these things may seem lacking to you. That being said, the focus is centered on the characters and their trial-some adventures of heroism. I hope you enjoy!

- Mason J. Schneider

In Loving Memory Of Socks

1 ELEVATOR 041

Bzzz! Bzzz!

"Time to get up!"

Bzzz! Bzzz!

Movement began to stir from somewhere deep beneath a warm comforter.

Bzzz! Bzzz!

"The early bird catches the worm!"

Bzzz! Bzzz!

The movement seemed to become more irritated as it thrashed from under the blankets on the bed, and after much struggle a curly brown mop of hair emerged from under the covers.

Bzzz Bzzz!

"Today has lots in store, let's get out of bed! Whaddya say pal?"

Suddenly the mop of hair extended out further to reveal the head of a young man, who looked quite annoyed by whatever had forced him to leave his current state of hibernation. He removed an arm from under the covers and slammed the top of a small device which was vibrating and flashing bright blue strobe lights around his room.

"Whaddya say we stop with the buzzing?!" the man asked irritably.

"Good morning Alfred! It's 7:00 p.m. Oh my... it appears you've slept all day!"

Alfred fixed his sleepy gaze on the metal egg-shaped device he had rudely slammed his hand on before. He took a moment to scratch his head and then let his arms reach up in a large stretch, yawning excessively.

"Oh yeah? And what's it to ya?" he muttered back to the egg.

"Well sir, it's no matter at all. But I thought perhaps I could inform you of an important date that has been set in your calendar?"

"Important date? What are you talking about Henry?" Alfred addressed the personal assistant by the name he had assigned it.

"Alfred I am pleased to inform you that your date with Cynthia is scheduled for tonight at 7:30 p.m. Shall I start the shower for you sir?"

"7:30? It's 7:00 o'clock Henry! You've just now decided to wake me up?"

"Not exactly sir. You slept through my first twelve alarms. And the time is now 7:05, shall I start that shower for you?"

"Twelve alarms...Cynthia...why did I have to pick a dating cruise to hide out on?" Alfred rubbed his hands against his eyes as he spoke.

"Yessir, Cynthia! Would you like me to read off her interests and description from the passenger files while you shower?"

"Forget the shower Henry, I don't have time. I've got to find something to wear." Alfred stood up out of bed and walked to the closet door in his room.

He clicked a button on the wall beside the metal door and the light on top illuminated in blue. The door slid up electronically into its frame.

"Alfred I would highly recommend you take a shower. My readings indicate your proper hygiene levels are extremely low."

"Yes, well I don't have time tonight Henry. Now help me pick out something to wear, and brew me a coffee."

An exasperated release of air sounded throughout the closet speakers.

"Henry." Alfred looked up to one of the many cameras in his closet which allowed the personal assistant to help him pick out clothes.

"Yes sir?" the A.I. asked nonchalantly. Its voice was slightly high pitched and sounded as if it was always trying too hard to be friendly- in Alfred's opinion.

"Did you just sigh at me? Is that what that whooshing was?"

"Exactly right sir! I found a soundboard filled with common humanoid noises. It was through my effort of sighing that I hoped to further my opinion that showering would be a healthy option for you!" the voice spoke as if it were delighted to inform Alfred the reasons behind its sighing.

"Henry, I promise to shower when I get back from my date tonight under one condition. Never, use that soundboard again."

"Okay sir. Now about that outfit! May I recommend outfit number 017?"

Alfred turned to look at the display screen in the center of the closet. It showed an image of the outfit on a model who looked much more physically fit than him and had a full beard. The man wore khaki pants with a plaid green and navy button up shirt, and a brown leather jacket over top.

"Henry, what did I tell you about leather jackets man?"

"Sir my records indicate you have informed me in the past that you don't believe you can pull off a leather jacket. However, my database has shown me that the jacket completes the look in this outfit, and if I do say so myself- looks quite well on the model in your display!"

"Yes Henry…" Alfred groaned as if he were exhausted at the thought of talking to the personal assistant any longer, "But that model looks like he just got done doing a hundred pushups and then fought a bear to cool down after his workout."

"Ha. Ha. Ha. You are too humorous sir! Bears have been extinct for three thousand and fifty-eight years. Ha Ha Ha." the robotic voice chuckled.

"I hate when you laugh like that Henry. I'll take the outfit, minus the jacket."

The display flashed in a green light to confirm Alfred's selection. The machine below it whirred and buzzed until a pair of folded khakis, underwear, and the button-up shirt shot out into a tray. A moment later the machine buzzed again and a belt and a pair of navy lace-up sneakers fell out as well. Alfred undressed quickly and threw his dirty clothes down a shoot in the closet. He put on his new outfit and then headed to the kitchen, where he grabbed a cup of freshly made coffee from underneath a dispenser. He took his cup and sat at a bar stool beside the kitchen counter. Alfred took a sip of his coffee and began to wake up a bit.

"Alfred, it's 7:20, you'll need to leave in the next fifteen seconds in order to make it to your date on time."

"There's nothing wrong with being fashionably late Henry. Only reason I'm even going is so I don't get kicked off this cruise yet, I'm supposed to be blending in."

The robotic voice spoke quietly and muffled through the surround speakers in the cabin, "Not exactly fashionable without the jacket."

Alfred looked up from his coffee, "Henry I know you did not just say that."

"Say what sir?" Henry chirped joyously back.

"Nevermind. Just be quiet while I drink my coffee. Please."

"As you wish sir."

Alfred took a few more sips of his coffee, enjoying the warmth from the cup in his hands.

"Alfred, I am pleased to inform you that you are officially a record holder aboard this ship!"

Alfred looked irritated that the voice had ignored his request for silence but asked anyway, "What are you talking about Henry? I haven't set any records."

"Actually sir, I have just completed a diagnosis of all the hygiene levels of every passenger on board the ship, and you have the lowest of them all!" Henry sounded elated to provide Alfred with this information.

Alfred stood up out of his stool and walked to the front door where he pressed a button identical to the one beside his closet. The light on top of the door flashed blue and then the door slid up into its frame.

"Good luck tonight sir!" Henry's voice sang out through the exit speaker.

"Piss off Henry." Alfred replied as he walked out of his cabin.

Alfred walked down a hallway that was surrounded by white metal walls and looked exceptionally clean. The floor beneath him was also white, although there were imprints where lights and signals would flash every so often. He passed by three more cabin doors before he reached an elevator. Alfred clicked the button beside the elevator door and waited. Nothing happened in the next couple of seconds to indicate that it was coming to pick him up. Alfred reapproached the button and this time pushed it in much more thoroughly with his index finger before stepping back. Another couple of seconds went by without any indication.

"Is this not working, what's going on?" Alfred said to himself as he walked back up to the button.

As he jammed his finger repeatedly on and off of it, he became enraged yelling- "Why won't you work damnit!"

A blue light flashed above the elevator and a cheerful voice, similar to Henry's but even more so thrilled, rang out from the speakers. "Hello there sir! I couldn't help but notice you seem a bit frustrated today, is there any way I could assist you?"

Alfred paused from his rage-clicking of the button and looked up at the blue light.

"Are you the goddamn elevator? Is that who's talking to me right now?" Alfred asked, obviously frustrated.

"Well yes of course I am sir- Elevator 041 to be exact!" the elevator responded.

"Then why the hell aren't you taking me up?" Alfred asked through gritted teeth.

"Sir, you have not yet commanded me to take you to any level on this ship. I cannot perform my functions without first being commanded by a passenger."

"What's your name?" Alfred asked, his face tight-lipped as he stared at the light above the elevator.

"My name sir?" the elevator responded as if it were confused by his question.

"Yes your name? You know, that thing people call you when they're addressing you?" Alfred explained irritably.

"I've already informed you. My name is Elevator 041. Pleasure to be at your service passenger!"

"Of course...of course it's just Elevator 041. Nevermind. What do you mean I didn't command you? I clicked that button a hundred times." Alfred argued.

"Yes sir, I saw that. However, the elevator assistant software recently updated and we now operate solely on voice command. Buttons are truly a technology of yester-year now, friend!" Elevator 041 happily explained.

Alfred took a moment and his cheeks puffed up with air before releasing in a long sigh.

"Elevator 041, please take me to floor fifty-six."

"Happy to serve you sir, step on in!" the elevator responded as its door slid open quickly.

Alfred walked into the spacious elevator and stood with his arms crossed. The door slid shut and the elevator began to make noises as it raised up slowly.

"I see you're going to floor fifty-six tonight, home of Shabby Dadoo's Intergalactic Water Food restaurant. That's one of the most expensive restaurants on board- excellent taste sir!" Elevator

041 broke the silence that Alfred had much been enjoying.

"Did you- did you say most expensive?" Alfred looked surprised to hear that the place he had picked was one of the most expensive onboard the ship.

"Correct! Shabby Dadoo's Intergalactic Water Food is not included on your passenger meal account, so looks like you'll be paying out of pocket for this one!"

"Not included, damn it. Damn the fine print. I only chose it because the food matched my date's preferences. Must be a picky eater." Alfred shook his head and furrowed his brow down as he spoke, obviously mad at himself.

"Sir would you like me to read your date's description and interests for tonight? We still have twenty floors to climb!"

"Yeah, okay. Whatever."

"Fantastic sir! I'll just need your first and last name in order to look up the date we have arranged for you this evening."

"Alfred Moreno." Alfred stated.

"Alfred Moreno." the electronic voice began, "It looks as if the Lonely Hearts Neptune Cruise has set up your nightly date with Cynthia Gwshkiftkaadarbis. Cynthia's interests incl-" Elevator 041 broke off as Alfred interrupted.

"What did you just say? What's her last name? Gwshkaftdu-what?" Alfred attempted to say the last name, completely butchering it.

"Gwshkiftkaadarbis." the elevator responded, pronouncing the last name perfectly which was something along the lines of:
Guish-Kift-Ka-Darbis

"That's a weird last name. Anyway go on with the interests." Alfred commanded the elevator, a hint of suspicion in his voice.

"Cynthia considers herself a bookworm- she's especially interested in books where the main character is a baby and is eaten by a monster in the end. She also enjoys watching films...Oh would you look at that- her favorite film is the classic "Baby-Eating SuperMonster: The Sequel. How wonderful! In addition to thi-" once again 041 paused as Alfred interrupted.

"What? What kind of joke is this? Babies getting eaten by monsters! That's horrible- who would watch or read anything about that? And sequel? How was there a sequel to a movie called Baby-Eating Monster?"

"I believe you mean Baby-Eating *Super*Monster." 041 joyously corrected.

Alfred stopped his rant for a moment and thought.

"Elevator, be honest with me. Is my date tonight a baby-eating monster alien from some weird planet?"

"I'm afraid I cannot answer race-related questions Alfred. The Lonely Hearts Neptune Cruise Line does not permit racism in any form." Elevator 041 explained.

"I'm not being racist. I just don't want to end up going on a date with a baby-eating alien! Is that really too much to ask?" Alfred seemed to be growing both angry and concerned as the elevator continued to rise.

"When you put it that way sir, you do seem to come off as a bit racist. My my... my sensors just completed a quick scan of your bias tendencies and I'm getting a 27% racist reading! For shame Alfred!"

"What, no! I am not racist, I just want to know what kind of person or uhh...creature I'm going to be going on a date with tonight." Alfred replied, quite alarmed that he was considered 27% racist.

"Why didn't you just say so sir?! We've only got five more floors to climb, so I'm afraid I don't have time to read off the remaining interests and description of Cynthia. However, I am delighted to inform you that Cynthia's arranged date from last night has left a comment on his feedback file. Isn't it great when passengers help passengers, Alfred?"

"Yeah, fantastic. Just read the comment."

"This comment was left by Darius Jordan, Cynthia's last recorded date onboard the cruise. The following was voice recorded by Darius himself- how wonderful! Playing recording:"

041's voice silenced, and what Alfred assumed was Darius' voice began to play through the speakers.

"Yo, I went on this date with this Cynthia broad...Damn! Let me tell you what- wildest night of my life man! We go to this weird ass restaurant that it says she recommended- somethin' like Shabby Dadoo or hell I don't know but it sounded crazy. So I was like shit let's get it! So I get to this restaurant and right off the bat- first thing I notice is that this lady definitely isn't human. I mean I'm talkin' seven foot tall green alien with mofuckin' tentacles, oozin' goo all over the table. But shit I ain't racist- so"

The recording broke off as Alfred begged the elevator, "Please. Just go back down. Take me back to my cabin."

2 FROM A.I. TO ALIVE

"Sir please, I urge you to listen to the remainder of the recording. We're only two floors away from Cynthia and you'll need this information to make your date a Slam-Dunk!"

"No...No. No. Just take me ba-" Alfred broke off as the Elevator spoke.

"Resuming recording."

"But shit I ain't racist so I go up, act all like a gentleman and such and as we sit down and have dinner I'm really starting to think this alien lady is kind of attractive. We havin' great conversations- I mean I don't understand anything she's sayin'- but hell the bartender kept pouring shots so I was having a great time! Well the dinner went pretty good- but then this shit got FUNKY! I start escorting the lovely lady back to my cabin- you know I was feelin' like tonight was my night. But soon as we get in there she whips out this freaky lookin' baby mask, and she's tryna put that shit over my face with those nasty tentacles drippin' goo all over the pla-"

"Elevator 041 I demand you take me back down at once!" Alfred looked to be quite distressed as he yelled angrily at the elevator.

"But sir, you know our policy that if you fail to appear for your scheduled date each night, you will be promptly kicked off the cruise!"

"I don't care- please just let me go."

"Oh look we've arrived- enjoy your date Alfred, and best of luck!"

The elevator door slid open and something prodded Alfred hard in the back, forcing him to stumble out of the elevator- which then quickly shut its door behind him.

"Really? You had to shove me out?" Alfred called behind him as a man wearing black dress pants, a white button up shirt, and a tie approached him holding a menu.

"Hello sir, I assume you are here for your arranged date this evening. What was the name?" he asked as a large smile spread across his face. His skin was riddled with acne and he had thin blonde hair falling all over different sides of his head.

"Uhhhhh..." Alfred hummed as he looked around the dining area, searching for his date.

A loud bang sounded from the right and as he turned and looked Alfred saw an extremely tall, green tentacled alien woman beating the lights out of a waiter holding a tray of food.

"Sir?" the waiter brought Alfred's attention back.

"Hold that thought." Alfred stuck his finger in the air as he replied and shuffled over behind some large decorative ferns that were planted in antiquely-ornate pots.

He poked his head up through the leaves to get a better look at the situation. Near the center of the restaurant there was a very nice bar, which was close to where he was supposed to be sitting. Alfred watched as the waiter who had been attacked by Cynthia was now kneeling before her and pleading for his life.

"I BEG YOU, PLEASE NO! The chef says we have no human baby here, and I don't know why your date is late, JUST PLEASE DON'T KILL ME!"

Cynthia appeared to pause for a moment, as if considering what to do next. By now the waiter who had greeted Alfred was getting involved.

"Madame, did you say you were looking for your date?" the waiter asked quickly, a bit of a French accent coming out.

"Don't do it man. Don't do it, come on." Alfred whispered to himself.

Cynthia roared, exposing a very strange mouth filled with bumps and long gooey tongue. A putrid smell began to fill up the room, and other people at the restaurant coughed as if it were poisoning them.

"I don't um...know exactly what that means ma'am, but perhaps you'd like to know that your date is here! He must be a little shy though because he's over there peeking up behind those ferns." the waiter continued, pointing directly at where Alfred sat crouched.

"You had to be that guy." Alfred cursed the man as he stood up quickly.

Cynthia turned and looked in his direction for the first time, and Alfred finally saw her face. Her head was what could be described as a cylinder of flesh, with two enormous black pits for eyes. Below these eyes were two slits, which Alfred assumed was her nose, and below these was the strange and disgusting mouth that had been revealed moments before.

"Hey there sweetie, sorry I'm late." Alfred addressed the baby-eating monster and looked at his wrist where no watch was present before continuing, "Oh would you look at the time- it's so late and I'm awfully worn out. I'll have to take a raincheck, so long! Farewell!" he spoke very quickly at the end and then dashed back towards the elevator.

"Somebody stop him, he's trying to ditch his date! He's banned from the cruise!" the waiter who had exposed Alfred previously was once again shouting, and once again ruining Alfred's day.

"Seriously man what the hell? Elevator 041 take me down! Quick!" Alfred yelled as he dove towards the door.

The door slid open and Alfred crawled in.

"Hello sir! How was your date? Did you manage to sneak off to hear the rest of the description recording? How smart! My my, you are brave Alfred!" 041 praised its passenger.

"Um the date was great! Short and sweet! Take me down. Now, please." Alfred explained quickly to the elevator.

The greasy-faced waiter was now rushing towards the open elevator door, followed by two more waiters behind him.

"What floor would you like to go to sir?" 041 asked pleasantly, seemingly unaware that Alfred was in an intense situation.

"Any of them, just not this one! CLOSE THE DOOR ELEVATOR 041!" Alfred was now yelling angrily.

The first waiter had by now made his way to the open door and was reaching his arms out as if to grab Alfred. Acting quickly, Alfred jumped back and kicked his right leg up and then out all in the same motion.

WHACK

The kick landed square on the waiter's face. He crumpled to the ground, his neck oddly bent, and groaned in pain. Just then Elevator 041 finally decided to slide shut its metal door. It slammed directly onto the ankle of the ugly waiter. Alfred heard the bone crack.

"AAAAAOOOOOUUU! GREAT GOD OF ASTROPHUS, AAAAAAGHH!" the waiter screamed in pain.

Alfred took his boot, the same one that had whacked the waiter in the face, and shoved his mangled foot out from under the door- which then shut the rest of the way. The elevator began to move. Alfred could tell it was going up by the force of motion below his feet.

"Resuming comment by Darius Jordan." 041 declared.

"No, I don't wa-"

"But damn she had a FAT ass. Whew lord!"

"End Recording."

Alfred let out a long sigh before speaking, "Elevator where are you taking me?"

"Since you gave me the fabulous duty of selecting your floor, I figured by default you'd want to go back to your room. But that's no fun, so we're going up to the top floor- Space Dome!" 041 answered happily, ending the word "dome" in an extremely high note.

"Wait no, take me down to my room just really fast so I can grab my stuff and then yes, we can go to the Space Dome!" Alfred offered.

"You got it sir!" the elevator responded joyfully.

"Yes! Yes, thank you!" Alfred seemed amazed that the elevator had listened to his command.

Suddenly Elevator 041 came to a halt. Then it dropped. Fast. Like two hundred miles per hour fast- directly downward. Alfred's body flew up and he smashed against the elevator ceiling before falling back down against the floor.

"Here we are sir! I'll keep the door open and ready for you." the elevator spoke as it slid its door open.

Alfred got himself up off the ground and ran out of the elevator and down the hall toward his cabin. He turned and crouched quickly around the corner wall of an intersecting hallway. Peering around, Alfred could see two guards running down the hall toward his cabin. He watched as they knocked on the door several times. Then one of the guards, a real buff guy with a massive chest and biceps, held up his hand. The other guard stepped aside as if to give the muscular man some additional room.

"Alfred Moreno," he began, speaking in a deep gruff voice, "You are hereby banned from the ship and if you continue to evade our staff we *will* open fire. Now open this Neptune forsaken door!" he finished with a shout and raised his leg in the air- slamming a large foot against Alfred's door and breaking it in.

"Well damn, he didn't have to go breaking doors down." Alfred laughed to himself.

The guards went inside Alfred's cabin and re-emerged a few minutes later.

"No sign of the passenger in his cabin. Over." One spoke into a walkie-talkie.

The man and his companion walked back down the hall in the opposite direction from the elevator. Seeing his window of opportunity, Alfred ran to his cabin and ducked inside the door frame quickly. He began to furiously open the drawers attached to his nightstand and then moved on to the mattress which he flung up off of its frame.

"Sir, I couldn't help but notice that you are back early from your date. Also, two men broke into your cabin. It appears you are being kicked off the ship."

"Yes yes, all a big mix up Henry. Have you seen that necklace I wear most of the time- you know the leather string one, with the shiny golden crystal in the middle of it?"

"Well of course sir, that's the one you always insist on wearing even though it never matches any of your outfits! It's in the safe, where you told me to keep it locked yesterday. That was just before you gave me my name!"

"Yes the safe! You're a genius Alfred." he complimented himself as he rushed over to the kitchen and opened the cupboards below the sink.

Inside there was an array of piping above what appeared to be a metal safe. Alfred punched in four numbers on a keypad and then turned the handle. Inside was the necklace he had been searching for. He grabbed it and quickly tied the leather string that was threaded through an amulet pendant around his neck. The amulet was made of a dark stone material, and the golden crystal in the center of it seemed to gleam with a glowing light. Alfred stood up and hurried over to his nightstand where he grabbed the metal egg-shaped device that Henry used to interact with him.

"Look Henry, I know you're going to hate me for this. But I might need your computing systems later, so looks like you're coming with me."

The egg began to flash blue from within Alfred's pocket.

"I agree to be taken hostage under one condition." Henry voiced.

"Satans of Saturn, what do you want?" Alfred demanded.

"Put on the leather jacket. Now that you are considered a fugitive on board the ship, you are finally badass enough to wear it!"

"You've got to be kidding me Henry."

"Jacket or I stay behind sir." the artificial intelligence sternly insisted.

"Ugh. I can already tell you're going to be a pain." Alfred mumbled as he ran to the closet and selected the jacket from the display. It shot out into the tray quickly and Alfred put it on.

"Happy now?" he asked as he ran out of the cabin and back down toward Elevator 041.

Henry said nothing, but flashed a few times in Alfred's pocket to show he was content.

As Alfred approached the elevator it lit up blue in excitement.

"Space Dome here we come!" 041 whirred excitedly.

Alfred ran into the elevator and the doors closed after him. It began to rise extremely fast, but not so much that it injured its passenger as it had before. As it continued to climb the levels of the spaceship, Alfred knelt on the ground and removed Henry from his pocket. He lifted up his shirt to reveal a strange knife hanging from his belt. He turned the egg upside down and pried at a latch on the bottom until it popped off.

"What are you doing to me sir? Why do you have a knife?" Henry sounded more curious than concerned.

"Just giving you a little upgrade Henry, don't worry about it."

"Ooo! An upgrade, aren't you lucky? I LOVE upgrades!" Elevator 041 chattered.

Within the egg a circuit board with an intricate wiring pattern could now be seen. In the center of the main panel was a green square, from which Alfred disconnected two small clamps. He then tossed the green square aside, and took his knife to the amulet around his neck, where he pried at the crystal in its center until it popped off. Quickly he attached the clamps to two sides of the crystal and replaced the panel he had popped off.

Alfred fell back as the entire egg began to glow with the same light that the crystal had been emitting. The light flashed bright and blindingly illuminated the entire elevator. Eventually it faded, and on the floor sat Henry's device- only now it was a polished bright gold color. Alfred walked forward, his face filled with awe, and then reached down and picked up the egg. Sure enough, the metal on the outside had become gold.

"Henry, how do you feel my man?" Alfred asked, wondering if the A.I. software had survived the overwhelming power of the crystal.

There was a short pause, during which Alfred began to feel slightly guilty, thinking he had killed the innocent software. But then the egg flashed an excited yellowish-gold light all around the elevator.

"I feel FANTASTIC! So many new calculations, so many more connections, every database is at my exposure! I have unlimited clearance across all sectors of information in the Universe! Curse My Circuits that jacket looks marvelous on you. Ohh yes, I don't know what you've done to me but I love it! Give me some more Alfred, more crystal! MORE CRYSTAL!!" Henry ranted on and on, his voice sounding as if it had even more energy behind it now than before.

"Calm down Henry, I can't have you getting all psycho on me. Now look, don't mention anything about the crystal I put in you. No one can know I have it. In return, you can keep it in you for awhile, and even once I remove it you will still feel the same as you do now. You no longer require a power source, as the crystal has essentially made you alive, or as alive as an A.I. can become I guess. Maybe I shouldn't have done that. You're not going to like enslave all of humanity now- are you Henry?"

"Of couurrseee not sir." the egg sounded incredibly pleased just to be talking, and its voice vibrated as if it were sitting in a massage chair.

"Gross." Alfred noted.

"We have arrived, SPACE DOME! Top floor!" Elevator 041, thrilled, announced.

Alfred grabbed Henry and tucked him inside of a pocket that was on the outside of his jacket. Meanwhile the elevator door had slid open. In front of Alfred were dozens of small space crafts all parked on one giant platform. Surrounding the entire platform was a massive dome enclosure. There were small orange circles all over the dome's surface where ships could be seen entering and leaving. The circle would open just long enough to let the length of the ship fly out or in, and then would snap sealed again. A large static noise played out across the dome. It soon cleared up into a voice being played through the shipyard's speakers:

"Attention! We are currently on the lookout for four fugitives. Three armed passengers, as well as one unrelated banned passenger, are approaching the Space Dome. Shoot on sight." it sounded as if the person speaking had the authority to command the guards to shoot someone.

3 ESCAPE OF THE LONELY HEART

Alfred ran out of Elevator 041 and into the mass of spaceships. He made it about a quarter of the way across before noticing one with an open entry-hatch. Quickly looking around he saw nobody near the door, but it looked as if the ship was about to take flight. There were blue energy rays coming from its propulsors and it was beginning to slowly levitate in place.

"What idiots would leave the door hatch open while taking off?" Alfred asked himself as he snuck inside the ship and hit the button to close the hatch behind him.

He walked up a short hallway and then climbed a ladder which led to the control room of the ship. As he pulled himself all the way up into the room, Alfred realized quickly he wasn't alone.

"Hey, who are you? You with the cruise?" Alfred turned to see that the nasally voice was coming from a stout and brawny creature which had the face of a man, but with two arms on each side rather than just one. Each one was muscular, but the bottom pair held a gun- which was now being pointed at Alfred.

By now the other two people in the control room had realized there was an intruder and moved over to where Alfred could see them. The first was a tall, slender woman who looked just a bit older than Alfred. She wore very advanced armor that appeared to be lightweight yet still durable and strong. It was made from an alloy that resulted in a metallic dark-red hue. She had black hair that curled below her shoulders and emerald green eyes that popped against the contrast of her olive-tan skin.

"Who the hell are you?" she asked, revealing a passionate voice, it commanded respect but Alfred thought he could hear a hint of kindness in it.

"I'm the other fugitive as you would have it, and say if you three were planning on making an escape here soon, I'd love to join in on the fun."

Her lips came together in a smile before she spoke, "You know how to fly a ship, fugitive?"

"I think I can work it out." Alfred replied with a grin.

The other stranger now spoke up, "Are you sure about this Marcie? Why should we trust this guy?" He was a human, as far as Alfred could tell. He looked to be about fifty or sixty, and had a balding head with bits of gray hair clinging to life in a circle around the edges. He wore baggy gray sweatpants, with a white tank top tucked into them. He too had some sort of machine gun pointed at Alfred.

Marcie, the woman in armor, replied sharply, "Because none of us know how to fly a ship, and we need to get the hell out of here as fast as we can. We'll keep a close eye on him, don't worry Jericho." She reassured the old man, who gave her a nod and lowered his gun while the four-armed man followed suit.

"Come on, the pilot's seat is this way." Marcie directed Alfred to follow her with a wave of her hand and he did.

She led him to the front of the room they were in, which had many control panels with flashing buttons and seats with straps attached to them. In the very front there were two chairs, similar to those behind them. Alfred took a seat in the pilot's chair and Marcie sat beside him.

"Do you really know how to fly this thing?" Marcie sounded as if she might have been regretting putting her trust in the stranger so quick.

Alfred was about to reply when a loud banging sounded from further below the ship.

"Open up! Out of the ship, NOW!" a voice yelled, and the banging continued.

Alfred acted quickly, pulling Henry out of his pocket and setting him in a nearby cup holder.

"Henry, connect to the ship and get us the hell out of here!" he ordered the A.I.

Henry flashed gold lights around the room and made a faint buzzing sound.

Moments later, the buzzing sound began to get louder, then even more so until it became hard to hear anything other than the vibrations pulsing throughout the ship. Suddenly lights illuminated all of the buttons on the main control dashboard. Henry had successfully hacked the ship. Alfred strapped himself into his chair, then pushed a metal lever up out of its resting place. The ship began to lift upward off of the ground.

"Better hold on tight, there's no way I'm skilled enough to time these exit circles. So we're going right through the dome!" Alfred explained to Marcie, and glancing down he noticed her hand was grasping his arm tightly as the ship rose rapidly into the air. He smiled to himself but said nothing.

As he spoke, she must have noticed that she was grabbing his arm, and moved her hand quickly back into her lap. Her hands, head, and face were the only parts of her skin that weren't covered in the red armor.

"What do you mean, *through* the dome?" she asked, her voice rising in alarm.

"Hang on back there!" Alfred yelled behind him to where the four-armed man and Jericho had taken seats.

Alfred pushed three different buttons, and then proceeded to force the lever farther up. He felt his body get thrown back in his seat as the spaceship blasted upwards in elevation even faster. The glass of the dome was quickly approaching and Alfred had a front row seat of it. Meters before the ship was about to meet the dome, Alfred pushed the lever even further up, and the ship thrusted forward- smashing through the glass. The hull of Alfred's ship was now badly broken, however no one was aware of that because everyone in the control room were now screaming in joy that they had somehow survived.

"Hell yeah! That's what I'm talkin' 'bout!" the four-armed man stood up and double fist-pumped the air with two of his arms. Then with the other two he raised his gun above his head and fired five rounds into the ceiling. A bullet ricocheted and hit the dash near Alfred.

"Hey easy back there, buddy. There's no reason to shoot a gun on this ship." Alfred turned and spoke to the man behind him as the ship continued forward into space, now controlled by Henry.

Just then another bullet bounced against the metal on the interior of the ship and whizzed past Marcie's hair. Two guards had somehow managed to make it on board, and they were firing rounds at the fugitives. Alfred tried to think of something to do, but before he could, the old man Jericho pulled out a stylish energy revolver and blasted three rounds directly into the forehead of the first guard. The bullet holes singed and smoke whispered out of his forehead. Alfred had a lot of experience with energy guns himself; they were a common weapon amongst those who required protection in the Universe.

The first guard's body dropped, and Alfred watched as the four-armed man grabbed an overhead pipe with two of his arms and then swung down onto the shoulders of the second guard. The guard looked up in surprise and tried to shoot, but was too late. The veins in the creature's muscular arms enlarged as he jammed the barrel of his gun into the forehead of the guard. Alfred cringed as he saw it break through the man's flesh, and couldn't imagine how strong the creature must be to be able to shove something through a man's skull. The creature pulled the trigger and three bullets rained out the backside of the guard's head.

Alfred thought he might throw up at the sight of it. He was beginning to taste his own saliva, and that almost always meant he was about to throw up.

"Seems like *that*, was a pretty good reason to shoot a gun on the ship." the four-armed man pointed out with a smirk.

Jericho simply laughed and nodded his head, and Alfred noticed he had his gray facial hair braided into two long strands with bands going all the way down each one of them. Alfred swallowed the spit in his mouth and took a deep breath. He felt a little less nauseous.

"Good job boys, and you too pilot." Marcie looked to her companions and then glanced at Alfred as she spoke.

"Hey no problem, what did I tell ya?" Alfred replied.

"Yeah yeah, so tell me- what's a young guy like you doing on an intergalactic lonely-hearts cruise? Have trouble getting the ladies?" she revealed a somewhat awkward laugh as she spoke.

Alfred took a moment before replying so that he could lower the lever that controlled the thrust of the ship. The spacecraft wasn't heading anywhere in particular. The temperature onboard had now increased by twenty or so degrees, due to part of the exhaust system getting destroyed when the ship had crashed through the dome. Alfred, feeling warm, unzipped his leather jacket and tossed it over his chair. The amulet necklace swung down around his neck overtop of his plaid shirt.

"Well, not that it's any business of yours but seeing as how you kind of helped me escape back there, I guess I'll let you in on a little secret."

"A secret?" Marcie didn't seem interested, and still hadn't looked over at Alfred.

"That's right. I'm a Rift Resolver. I just got done securing an important artifact, and I was laying low on that crui-" Marcie stood up out of her chair as she interrupted Alfred's explanation.

"You, you're a Rift Revolver?" she asked, shocked.

"Well yeah, why so surprised?" Alfred laughed.

"It's just I've only ever heard of them. Members of a secret society who absolve eddies and lapses in time in order to keep the Universe in proper working order. That's you?"

"Wow, you chock it up to be a whole lot more than most people. Maybe I'm cooler than I think." Alfred joked.

Marcie's eyes now dropped to Alfred's chest, where she saw something she never in a million years would have expected to see.

"Is-is..that? Could it really be?! GOSIA'S AMULET?" she shouted out in disbelief.

Jericho and the four-armed man stepped forward to look for themselves. Alfred attempted to cross his arms over his chest before they could see, but it was too late.

"My Goddamned Galaxies, it is Gosia's Amulet! Give it up now, Rift boy!" Jericho spoke up and once again raised his gun to point at Alfred.

"Gosia's Amulet? GOSIA's Amulet? GOSIA'S AMULET!" the four-armed man began to jump up and down, screaming in excitement as he pounded his fists like an animal against the floor.

"Everybody just calm down now." Alfred began, standing up and putting his arms above his head. There were now two guns being pointed at him. "Yes, it is the amulet. However, I must return this to the god Gosia soon, otherwise there's going to be a lot of drastic changes occurring throughout the Universe."

"Too bad." Marcie began, she extended her arm, making some sort of movement which forced a sharp blade to slide out of the end. She took her bladed arm and sliced the leather necklace clean off of Alfred, and grabbed it with her other hand before it could fall to the floor. "Rumor had it that someone on that ship was in possession of the Amulet. Who would have thought that the man who helped save us would turn out to be in possession of the very item we were hired to steal!"

"Ha ha! Yes, yes- now that we have the Amulet we should get back to the boss as soon as possible. He will be pleased with your work." Jericho advised Marcie.

"Of course. Tie him up Fusnic, and calm down-quit pounding the floor." Marcie ordered the four-armed man.

Fusnic continued to pound the ground and Alfred saw what looked to be foam frothing out of his mouth.

"Give me the AMULET! I must have its powers. I MUST!" Fusnic charged in a furious rage towards Marcie, who quickly tossed the necklace in the air over to Jericho.

Jericho caught it instinctively then yelled out, "What the hell did you do that for? Now he's coming for me!"

The old man tried to pull his gun from where it was strung over his shoulder, but Fusnic had turned and was now approaching fast. Jericho must have decided he wouldn't have had enough time to shoot, so he jumped and slid down the ladder in the control room-leading back near the entry hatch. Alfred was impressed that the old man could move so quickly for his age. Thinking he better do something before this all turned out very bad, Alfred took the moment while Marcie was distracted and brought his elbow down hard on top of her head. She began to fall, unconscious, but Alfred caught her body and sat her down in a chair.

"Sorry...sorry! You're really hot by the way. Okay good talk." he apologized to the passed-out girl as he ran by her.

Alfred headed for the ladder where Fusnic had just leaped down to chase after Jericho. Now all three of them were in the entry bay of the ship. Alfred watched, slightly in horror, as he saw the old man clinging to the side of the hatch door, which had been opened by Fusnic. The same hand that clung for his life also held the amulet necklace in its grip. Alfred couldn't move any closer or he'd get sucked out of the ship with the blasting air that was caused by the open hatch. Fusnic was gripping a different overhanging pipe with each arm. He moved forward easily, grasping one pole then the next as if he were on a playground. Soon enough he was right above Jericho's hand.

"You foolish beast! We could have all just shared the Amulet's powers; you would have gotten your body back to normal had you been patient!" the old man yelled through the blasting air being sucked out of the moving ship.

"The Amulet or you die." Fusnic hissed through clenched teeth.

"Then death it'll be. Damn you to hell beast!" he shouted while simultaneously letting go of the side wall- getting sucked into space with the Amulet still in his grip.

"No! You didn't have to-" Alfred's cries cut short as he watched Fusnic release his grip on the bars to go after the Amulet and get blasted out of the ship as well.

Alfred carefully edged along the side of the wall until he reached a button and clicked it to close the hatch.

"What a mess. It'll probably make my job easier though. Still, they didn't have to die." Alfred spoke to himself as he climbed back up the ladder to the main control room.

He rolled up the sleeves of his shirt as he sat back in the pilot's seat. Beside him Marcie still remained unconscious. Alfred took a moment to strap her safety belts in a way that she would be constrained when she woke. Then he looked to Henry who still sat in the cupholder.

"Sir?" Henry asked, sounding uncertain.

"To Jenni's Roller-Rink, just above the planet Cistron."

"You got it sir!" Henry could hear the confidence in his companion's voice returning, and this cheered him up. The egg flashed gold lights around the room and the damaged ship took off at high speed into deep space.

4 TEA-BOT

Alfred could feel his eyes growing heavier each time he closed them to blink. Just as he was beginning to drift into a light sleep, he woke with a start as Marcie shouted beside him.

"Hey what...where... YOU HIT ME!" Marcie seemed confused at first but her eyes lit up with rage when she saw Alfred. She struggled against the straps that Alfred had fashioned to keep her from getting out of the chair.

"Yes, and I'm very sorry about that. But hey, at least you're not dead like those other guys!" Alfred joked.

Marcie's eyes widened in shock as she proclaimed, "Dead? What do you mean dead? Where's Fusnic and Jericho?"

Alfred realized that was probably the worst way ever to tell someone their two companions had just died. Oh well, he thought, they did all try to steal the crystal and kill me- must be karma.

"Yeah those guys...Yup they're dead all right. The old man got sucked into space and the crazy four-armed thing jumped out after him. Forgot you were on their side for a sec." he added nonchalantly.

When Alfred finished speaking Marcie took a deep breath before she replied.

"But how could you let the Amulet get lost, didn't you need to return it so that the Universe continued to flow as normal? I don't understand."

"Well, you guys were more knowledgeable than I thought you'd be on precious universal artifacts, but you got one minor little detail mixed up. Or hey, maybe I just have the inside scoop!" Alfred smiled to himself. He liked to feel important.

"And what's that?" Marcie asked, more curious now than anything.

Henry joined the conversation, "It's Gosia's *Crystal* that is the actual artifact. The amulet is simply a placeholder for it to sit on. It is a shame though, that amulet was made from Rodinium, an incredibly rare ore that we could have sold for enough currency to fix the major damages on this spacecraft."

"First of all, why is that egg talking? And second, I assume that means you have the crystal still, and let my greedy gunmen die over essentially nothing?" Marcie asked, no emotion in her tone.

"Well I couldn't really have saved them without getting sucked out myself. So yeah, that about sums it up. And oh, that's Henry. He's the one steering the ship and *also* the one who just now mentioned the fact that it has major damages." Alfred replied, glaring at the egg which lit up a moment later as if in spite.

"Well I'm not that mad, those two were just going to get in my way. Surprised they didn't get themselves killed before this to be honest. I was planning on double-crossing them once I had the amulet, I mean *crystal*, anyway."

"That's pretty heartless," Alfred laughed, "so what's your story?"

"Pardon me! Pardon me, before you begin your story Miss Marcie, I'd like to make you both aware that I have located the kitchen-robot staff members, and one is still functional. Tea-Bot is on its way to assist you with your beverage needs!" Henry interrupted.

"That's great Henry." Alfred returned sarcastically.

A strange shuffling noise could be heard from farther away in the ship. Marcie and Alfred exchanged a suspicious look, but dismissed it to being whatever Henry was talking about.

"Well technically I'm working for my boss, a man by the name of Sham-Bon. He is the current head of the Huck Family, in other words a king on my planet. But the royal family has very little legitimate influence on the politics of Hemphion, and Sham-Bon is out to change that. Our job was to steal Gosia's Crystal. He claimed he could use it to save our planet from its sun- which is believed to be dying out and will explode in a matter of years. Well, the king somehow came to learn that the Crystal was somewhere in an underwater cavern-maze on the planet Zuptraph. So he sends a group of his men to find it, but apparently just as they reached the center of the maze, they looked up to see someone else swimming away with it. They chased after him but he disappeared in a flash of light."

"Did they mention anything about him being extraordinarily handsome?" Alfred butted in.

"I realize now it was you. So Sham-Bon, who also happens to be the man that helped me to survive once my parents died, hires me to retrieve the Crystal for him. He received a tip that a man with a strange knife had checked into a nearby space cruise, and I guess he must have assumed it was a member of the Rift Society who had taken the crystal from the maze. But he didn't tell us that part."

"And what made *you* qualified to steal a universal artifact from a Rift Resolver?"

"Sham-Bon paid for me to have the very best training." Marcie replied coolly.

"Training in what?" Alfred asked, curious.

"I'm the best assassin this side of the galaxy."

"HAHA, you? An assassin?" Alfred was grabbing his waist with his arm, bent over in his chair laughing hysterically.

"Why the hell is that so hard to believe?" asked Marcie, quite visibly pissed off.

"Well it's just I sorta knocked you out really easily." Alfred said, rubbing the back of his head.

"Whatever. Anyway, Sham-Bon claimed he was stealing the Crystal in order to get Hemphion a new sun. But overtime I've begun to see signs of much darker intentions, such as conquering other planets and expanding the rule of the Huck Family even further. So I decided to continue to play along and I was go-"

"You were going to steal it and use it to save Hemphion yourself, because you don't trust this Sham-Bon guy."

"That's right." she replied; her eyes sincere. "I don't know exactly what he plans on doing with the Crystal of Gosia if he gets his hands on it, but I know it won't be good. I don't even know if he seriously intends on trying to save Hemphion or not. That's why you *have* to tell me where it is. The people throughout the rural villages of my planet are all that's left besides the Huck Family. Parliament declared an official evacuation years ago and most everyone in the major cities fled to far-off planets. It's too late for my people to leave now, they won't be able to get out of the radius of the sun's effects in time. Besides, most villages have even begun to put their faith in the king, seeing no other sign of hope. My village alone still stands against him."

"Well, and no offense, I'm not going to tell you where the crystal is- but maybe we can work something out. Believe it or not, I'm actually not a huge fan of evil kings and exploding planets myself." Alfred rubbed his bare chin as if he had a beard and was thinking something over.

The shuffling noise in the background was growing steadily louder, but still sounded far-off in the ship.

"I can't negotiate this. I must return with the crystal." Marcie looked steadily at Alfred with her emerald eyes.

"You're not really in a place to negotiate." Alfred began, pointing at how her arms were strapped to the chair she sat in. "But tell you what, you help me out on a couple little errands I have to run, and when I return the Crystal to Gosia I'll have him use his power to save Hemphion. Deal? Whaddya say?"

"And you expect me to believe that a God is just going to do *you* a favor?" Marcie asked in disbelief.

"Well yeah. I'm a Rift Resolver. I'm doing Gosia a favor by retrieving his crystal, and in return he can do me the favor of creating a new sun for your world. Plus, he hasn't had the full extent of his powers without the crystal- so I know he'll be wanting it back pretty bad. I'm a universal problem-solver remember? Besides, me and Gosia have met a few times before."

"You're *friends* with a God? You're only like twenty-something."

"Haha, you're too kind sweetheart. Rift Resolvers travel all throughout space and time, my dear Marcie. I think the last time I added it all up I came out to be around five hundred and thirty one years old. But yes, if we're talking about my body's age I'm twenty-two. So what do you say, you help me and I help you?"

Marcie continued to look somewhat stunned, but she must have believed Alfred for she said, "Deal. And I'm calling you Al from now on."

Alfred just sat back in his chair and offered her a smile.

"Where are we headed anyway?" Marcie asked, smiling back slightly.

"Jenni's Roller-Rink!" Henry answered in delight.

"Roller-Rink, what? Why?"

Alfred pulled his knife from his belt. It was very odd looking, the blade was made from a sort of purple stone-like material, and it swung out of a white handle which appeared to be made of bone. Alfred cut the straps restraining Marcie as he replied.

"That's right, we've got a date." Al winked and rubbed his hand playfully on the top of Marcie's hair.

For the next two hours they both tried to catch up on their sleep as Henry piloted what remained of the ship toward Jenni's Roller-Rink. The shuffling noise continued to become gradually louder, but it still wasn't close enough to wake either of the passengers.

***

Bzzz Bzzz

"Alfred we have arrived."

Bzzz Bzzz

Alfred didn't sleep past this alarm; his senses were back to being on full alert now that he was on a mission. He shook Marcie's arm until she too was awake. Henry had landed the ship on a medium-sized parking lot outside of what looked like a teen-hangout from the 1950's. A bright neon billboard lit up the sky in pink, reading: **Jenni's Roller-Rink**. Alfred stood up out of his chair and stretched.

"What the hell is that sound?" Marcie asked irritably.

Shhherft Shhherft

"It's probably this damn ship, I doubt we'll even be able to get this thing back up in the air." Alfred replied.

"Why are we here again?" Marcie asked, confused.

"Follow me. Henry, you're going in my pocket." Alfred answered as he grabbed the golden egg and put it in the pocket of his jacket.

Al led the way down the ladder and out the exit door hatch, which he closed after Marcie followed him out. She held his arm as they ran toward the entrance of the Roller-Rink. Lights of many colors could be seen flashing through the windows. Back inside the spacecraft a noise sounded in the main control room.

Shhherft Shhherft

A small white robot shuffled up the ladder. It dragged itself using only its arms until its body sat on the floor. Its legs were completely missing and one could see where many wires and metal components hung off from where they had once been attached. On its forehead there was an imprint of a leaf, which glowed bright green as the little robot spoke for the first time in a very long time.

"Did someone request tea?" he asked the empty room, looking from side to side.

His chest panel swung open and a dispenser was revealed with a cup sitting on a tray below it. Hot green tea flowed out of the robot and overfilled the small white cup, which fell to the floor spilling all over the ground.

Tea-Bot attempted to move but slid in the spilled tea and fell hard against the floor. The exposed wires that touched where the tea had spilled sparked and electrocuted the small white robot. A fire ignited in the main control room.

It spoke one last time, as the green leaf on its forehead slowly dimmed out.

"Enjoy."

The electric fire grew larger and larger until it reached the fuel bay of the spacecraft- making the entire thing explode in a cloud of flames.

5 JENNI'S ROLLER-RINK

Alfred swung open a large glass door, and gestured for Marcie to walk in first. Inside was a massive roller-rink, with tons of people rollerblading all over. There were silver bleachers that ran all around the length of the outside of the ring. Here, several people sat and watched, but most were on the platforms in front of these seats. These people danced and cheered for the rollerbladers.

BOOM

"Hey, did you hear something?" Al asked Marcie.

"No, I can't hear anything over this music!" she replied, trying hard to shout overtop of the song that was currently being blasted through the speakers.

Alfred shrugged and led Marcie over to a countertop to their right. Behind it leaned an older gentleman who wore a suit and tie. He had a big nose and long white hair that he had pushed back on top of his head, making him look like an elegant mad scientist.

"Al Moreno! How long's it been? Come here son, give me a hug, get ova' here!" the man spoke in one of those accents where you always felt obliged to do whatever it was he was asking.

"Papari, it's good to see you old man!" Alfred reached across the bar and the two exchanged a hug over the countertop. Papari patted him on the back excessively before they let go- that's just the kind of guy Papari is.

"And who's the lovely lady in the red armor?" Papari asked Al, turning to smile at Marcie.

"This is Marcie, she's a friend helping me out with some Rift business." Al introduced her, and Marcie and Papari shook hands. Papari held her arm for a second, staring at the armor that enclosed her limbs.

"That's Altarian Rue Armor! Now how in Jupiter's Jawbreakers did you get your hands on that?" Papari looked up, letting go of her arm.

"Let's say it came to me by chance." Marcie made it seem as if she didn't want to discuss the origins of her armor.

"Fair enough young lady, I'm not one to snoop!" Papari laughed and turned to Al who seemed puzzled by the interaction that had just occurred, "I assume you're here to talk to someone in the Society?"

"That's right."

"Well look, that's no problem at all. But the only one down there right now is Aaron Flux."

"Damn it, it had to be Flux...Ugh- I guess he might be able to help us out. Hey old man, open the secret gate, will ya?"

"You got it Al. Hey, how's about giving the folks a show while you're here, like the good old times? When ya was just a little guy."

"Just for you old man, sure thing. Besides, I wanna see if Marcie's got any fun in her at all."

Papari reached under the counter and pulled up a pair of men's rollerblades. Alfred took them over to a nearby bench and began to put them on.

"What size ya need sweetie? And hey Al, show me your Rift Blade, you know the protocol!"

Alfred reached to his belt and held up the enclosed knife he had used to cut Marcie free earlier.

Papari gave him a thumbs up and Marcie replied, "Give me a nine."

Papari reached back down and grabbed her rollerblades and wished them both a good time. Once they had on their wheels, they headed over to the gate to get into the rink.

"I'll open the gate when ya get done with the finale!" Papari called to them as they stepped out onto the floor.

Marcie held onto Al at first as they rolled to the right with the flow of the other creatures and people going by. Surround speakers must have made up every part of the ceiling, except where there was a disco ball or shining neon spotlight. A funky techno pop song played.

Marcie let go of Alfred's arm and began to roll in time to the music. For a moment it almost looked like she was enjoying herself.

"You have horrible, horrible taste in music. But you can blade baby, no doubt about it!" Al complimented and insulted her at once.

They slowed down and watched as a creature that resembled an ostrich rolled by lightning fast. He was upside down, and was balancing his head on a single rollerblade boot- while his feet kicked madly around in the air.

"Jeeze, people take this seriously." Marcie said to Al as they continued to roll towards the middle of the rink.

"You have no idea who you're talking to. Get ready to see a level of rollerblading you never even thought existed."

"Okaaay then." Marcie thought Al was joking, but his face was serious.

Suddenly, as they were nearing the middle of the rink, the techno music stopped. And with the music everyone rollerblading, dancing, and cheering eventually paused as well. A voice came on over the speakers and all the lights dimmed.

"Ladies, Lifeforms, and everyone in between! We've got something special for you all tonight!" it was Papari talking, "Please clear the floor for the Master Rift Rollerblader, King of the Rink, Al Morenoooo!" as he finished everyone in the crowd remained silent for a moment.

Then a spotlight shined on Al, as well as Marcie, and someone from the bleachers shouted, "Oh my stars, that *is* Al Moreno, ooouu!" The whole place went wild.

An elegant classical song came on over the speakers as the floor cleared and Al and Marcie rolled to the middle. The crowd continued to applaud them. Al put one arm on Marcie's armored waist and took her other hand in his.

"Alfred I'm an assassin; I don't really know how to rollerblade! What even is all *this*?" Marcie whispered fiercely to him.

"Hey calm down, it's going to be fun! You should have a great sense of balance and speed. Just follow my lead and when the finale ends go to the middle of the rink where Papari will open the gate."

"What, no! I hate being the center of attention Alfred!" but he had already begun to rollerblade out onto the floor, dragging Marcie with him until she cooperated.

The spotlight followed them as Alfred led Marcie through a very elegant dance, one which brought several creatures to tears in the crowd. Al noticed Marcie was smiling. The gentle music began to fade away and a really upbeat jazz number came on. Alfred picked up the pace and spun Marcie all around the rink. At one point she even rollerbladed between his legs, incredibly fast, and came back up- sticking the landing! The crowd loved it and cheered accordingly.

Eventually the jazz began to die down and a loud bass started to boom throughout the rink. Marcie looked at Al as if to say "What now?"

"Just head to the very center, I'll meet you there. Great moves by the way!" Alfred yelled through the intensifying music.

To the right of the center of the floor, platforms were electronically sliding away and four objects rose up from below the rink. The first three were hoops that were held in the ground by posts. The fourth was a ramp- and quite a tall one at that. The hoops were in descending heights- so that the closest one to the end of the ramp was the highest, and the last one was the shortest and landed near the middle of the floor.

Alfred listened to the crowd roar in applause as he made his way to the top of the ramp via a platform in the floor that lifted as he rolled onto it. When he got to the top he paused and blew kisses from each hand into the crowd. They couldn't get enough of him. Just then, the outside rings of the hoops were illuminated in fire. The crowd oo'd and awe'd. Marcie looked a bit concerned and moved farther away from the flame's reach.

"Sir, you realize I'm still in your pocket?" Henry spoke up from inside Al's jacket, he sounded frightened.

"To be honest I totally forgot, but it's too late now- hang on Henry!" and with that Al let his body weight lean him forward and he began to roll down the ramp.

If someone in the crowd blinked during those next few seconds- they would have missed it all. Alfred flew off the curved ramp and went soaring up toward the high ceiling. Marcie watched as he flipped in the air and somehow caught the golden egg that slipped out of his jacket pocket while he was upside down. While doing so, he went through the first fiery hoop. By the second he was halfway back to being right side up. And through the third he managed to swing his body the rest of the way around- landing on his feet and rolling steadily over to Marcie.

"Al Moreno everyone!" Papari announced to the crowd, who in turn cheered louder than they had all night.

Marcie and Al rolled over to the middle, and from somewhere in the floor a dense smoke started blasting out.

Alfred coughed a little as he explained and took off his skates; indicating for Marcie to do the same, "So no one sees."

He led her to a square shape that had opened up in the middle of the floor. Marcie peered down and her armor formed new red metal boots around her feet.

"Wow, that's handy. Ladies first." Al said as he followed her down in just his socks.

The floor closed back behind them a few moments later. Lights had been turned on and ran overhead every few steps they walked down. Al slid past his companion to lead the way into the depths of Jenni's Roller-Rink.

"So you run around fixing things in the Universe, and on the side you're a um...professional rollerblader?" Marcie couldn't help but laugh a little as she spoke.

"Pshht, not professional. But yeah I got pretty good here as a kid. Jenni's Roller-Rink has been here ever since I can remember. It was built as a cover-up for the Rift Sanctum below- a.k.a. where we're heading."

"So where was Jenni? Oh no, she hasn't passed away has she? And why were you here as a kid?" Marcie asked, nervous that she might have struck a sore spot.

"No, no. Haha! Jenni is Papari's wife, and she's usually in the back office doing paperwork. You see, Papari was in the Rift Society a long, long time ago. But he only stayed in for a few years. Something happened to him one day I guess. He saw something he insists to this day he can't even speak about on the planet Dorphnok. So he left the Society as a Rift Resolver but stays on as an honorary member. Him and his wife opened this roller-rink above the Sanctum a few years after he left. As for me, I've never known my real parents and those two actually found me here as a baby. They took care of me and so I never really questioned the exact circumstances. I was just grateful for what they did for me. With the Sanctum right below me as a kid I was seeing a lot of

Rift Society members, and the day I turned eighteen I went off to join the training academy."

"I see. It must have been a hard life without knowing your real parents." Marcie sounded as if she could relate to Al's past.

Alfred said nothing regarding her comment but instead announced "Just a few more steps, we're almost there. And don't let this Aaron Flux guy get to you he's kind of-"

"Kind of amazing, handsome, fiersome, heroic? Which one was it that you were going to say, Al old pal?"

They had walked down into a massive underground room. There were all sorts of strange equipment and devices and artifacts spread out on lab tables around the outside. In the center there were several brown leather couches and chairs as well as a large monitor that sat on a stand in front of them.

"I was going to say he's kind of a... Jackass." Alfred finished.

"Why thank you Alfred, I thought you were going to insult me!" Aaron Flux replied, quite surprised.

"He did. He just called you a Jackass." Marcie spoke up, now getting a good look at Flux.

He looked to be about the same age as Al, but he was a few inches taller and had dark black hair that was combed neatly back. He had blue eyes that bordered on a violet hue and wore a long-sleeved shirt made of an elastic material.

"Precisely! I thought he would have called me a lion or a shark. Or something else laughable and weak! But the Jackass was one of the fiercest predators during the third millennium- they were said to have been outranked only by the Argentine Lake Duck on the food chain!"

Marcie glared at Aaron for a moment and then looked at Al.

"I don't think that's right…" she said slowly.

"And you are, other than stunningly gorgeous?" Flux asked, trying to pull away one of Marcie's hands as if to give it a kiss.

Alfred gulped as he saw the look change to fury in her eyes. Quickly she moved her arm upwards, smacking Flux hard across the face and leaving him shocked, holding his head in his hands.

"Marcie." she answered, regaining her composure as quickly as if she had just swatted an irksome gnat away from her face.

"Wow you really do like the feisty ones, don't ya Moreno?" Aaron had stood back up. His cheek looked bright red where it had been smacked.

"Aaron just shut up; I need to talk to you about something." Al began.

"Yes, yes, what brings the wandering Resolver back to thy humble Sanctum?" Aaron joked, sitting down in one of the leather armchairs. He picked up a remote and clicked something on it, making the monitor turn on. A planetary news show was being broadcasted. A human woman wearing a red button up suit was sitting behind a newsroom counter. In the top right of the screen was an image of what looked like a sun.

"We bring you live footage of the planet Hemphion- where scientists say that the planet will overheat and be comple-" Alfred quickly grabbed the remote and turned off the monitor.

Aaron looked at Al as if to say, "What the hell man?" but Al just shoved Aaron's arm and mouthed out the word "idiot" to him. Al looked over expecting to see a crying or enraged girl in red armor, but Marcie was just now sitting down in a chair across from him and didn't look like she had heard anything. Alfred sat down, relieved.

"Alright look Flux, I have the crystal- now I just need to get to Gosia. I wasn't briefed on exactly how to get there and the only other times I've had to deal with Gosia he came to our dimension. Do you know how I can reach him?"

"Whaaaat! They gave *you* The Crystal of Gosia case? I put in for that one forever ago, and they said I wasn't intelligent enough to talk to a God like Gosia. That he wouldn't appreciate my personality- can you believe that?" he looked at Al in disbelief.

"No way! You?" Marcie replied, letting the rudeness come out in her voice.

"Yes, look Flux- just tell me how to get to Gosia." Alfred was getting impatient.

"It's simple my friend. You take a possession of the god you'd like to pay a house call to- in this case it's Gosia's Crystal. Then you, being a Rift Resolver, take your Rift Blade and stab down directly in the center of the object. It won't damage the crystal- it being the possession of a god it would take a lot more than that. Anyway, that'll open a portal for you to travel to see old Gosia."

Just then Henry spoke up, and Alfred removed him from his jacket pocket and set him on the table between Al and Aaron.

"STAB? What is he saying Alfred? Sir, you wouldn't stab me would you? Oh Motherboard, Oh Have

49

Mercy, sweet mother of my sacred circuits." he ranted in a panicked voice, flashing his golden lights all over the room.

"Woah...what the hell is that?" Aaron put his hands in the air and scooched away from where Al had set Henry.

"It's the crystal. Which happens to be connected to my A.I. Henry here. The crystal permanently enhanced him, basically giving him life and allowing him to be a sort of super intelligent program that can connect to databases and technology throughout the universe. But since I haven't removed the crystal yet he's been really annoying and talkative because of all the extra energy. Well he's pretty annoying no matter what, but you know." Al explained.

"You mean the crystal's been in that thing this whole time?" Marcie looked at Alfred in surprise.

"Since when have you had an A.I. though, Moreno?" Flux asked, looking confused.

"Since I stole Henry from that cruise I was laying low on after I got out of the maze on Zuptraph." Al explained.

"Nice man! Most of the time I just take the little shampoo bottles and the pens from hotels, but the hyper-intelligent A.I. you got was a good choice too!" Aaron seemed genuinely impressed.

"Alright well it was nice seeing you and all Aaron, but I'm visiting Gosia and getting this over with. Stay here with Marcie until I get back, it shouldn't be long."

Marcie stood up, "Make sure you get Hemphion a new sun Alfred. Please."

Aaron's eyes grew wide and his mouth opened a little. He looked at Alfred who was dismantling Henry and removing the crystal from his circuit board.

"So you- you're from Hemphion then, I'm um assuming?" Aaron asked Marcie, not looking at her.

"Yes." Marcie replied.

Aaron was beginning to realize why Alfred had shut off the monitor earlier, but being the idiot that he was he announced the following:

"Haha! Al, remember a few months ago when we had that Rift meeting and everyone got hammered and that news broadcast came on talking about Hemphion getting destroyed so you started making a bunch of explosion noises an-" Alfred tried to cut him off but Aaron didn't notice and continued, "and you were saying *hey look everybody guess who I am? Boom! BakOOOM! Bwaaahh! I'm Hemphion gettin' my shit blown up!* And then everyone laughed and cheered haha, good times."

Alfred turned and looked at Marcie, who was shaking with anger in her seat. Alfred walked up towards Flux who had begun to continue his story:

"And then you were like *Oh no! My sun, my sun! Oh my crust is melting oo-*"

BAM!

Alfred swung a right fisted uppercut and landed it under Aaron's chin. Flux fell to the floor, clearly knocked out.

"Look Marcie I'm so-" Al began.

"If you want to show me that you're really sorry you'll do whatever you can to try and get my planet a new sun." Marcie interrupted and turned away from Alfred with tears in her eyes.

"I will, I promise." he looked at her, filled with guilt and anger at himself for saying such terrible things. He hadn't meant them, not in the slightest. It's just that he had gotten really drunk and everyone was saying ridiculous things to entertain each other. Still, he had learned a valuable lesson- don't let Marty from the Society mix your gin and tonics.

Al Moreno pulled his Rift Blade once again from his belt and disattached the clamps that connected Henry to Gosia's Crystal. He put Henry back in his jacket pocket and the egg let out a long sigh of relief now that the crystal had been removed. Henry was glad that he had been given the rare opportunity to be one of the few A.I.'s who were genuinely alive, and he decided he would stick by Al Moreno's side to thank him for his eternal gift. Alfred placed the Crystal of Gosia on a lab table and raised his Rift Blade high above his head. He looked over at Marcie once more.

Rift Blades are rare universal tools that have been used by Rift Resolvers for eons. Each one is crafted from different rare materials, and an individual who trains in the Society receives his Blade and its powers when he graduates the program. The Rift Blade can slice through space- creating a split (or rift) in the Universe itself. However, a Resolver can only open a rift to a location he has been to before. Even then, the rift will only become a successful portal if it is the true will of the Universe, hence this is why these individuals are truly considered the acolytes of the Universe. The Rift Resolvers use these blades to travel to the necessary places in space in order to change certain courses of events that if left to play out themselves would lead to more harm and unnecessary destruction. Some say that Rift Society members are people who take on the role of gods or the Universe themselves. However, the Society always regards these complaints with the same mantra:

The Universe is all-knowing. Every event in history has long been known and scripted by the All-Knowing. Thus, when a Resolver is able to open a Rift in space, it was truly already the will of the One for it to be opened. And the actions taken by Society members that prevent events from happening follow the same principle- if the attempt by a Resolver is successful it was meant to be. Likewise, if the event occurs regardless of a Resolvers attempt to stop it- the occurrence must have certainly been the choice of the Universe itself. Thus is why every member of the Society endures years of training- in order to adapt their moral compass and life energy to follow the One's will.

In order to be used properly, a Rift Resolver must use the skills they perfected over many years of training to force their own inner energy into the blade of the knife at just the right moment- in order to travel to their point of interest. This is part of the reason why some Rift Resolvers are so famous around the Universe regardless of the location they go to.

Alfred closed one eye and concentrated on the center of the crystal with his other. He focused his inner energy and allowed it to combine with the Divine Energy- what Resolvers call the energy of the Universe. Then he slammed his blade down into the dead center of Gosia's Crystal. All the while he focused on three things.

Gosia. Marcie. Getting a new sun for Hemphion.

6 "WHAT A TRIP!"

For a split-second Alfred felt incredible. It was as if
the crystal was lending him its power. Then there was
nothing but darkness and he wondered if he had died.
Flux wasn't the brightest after all, and he might have
gotten the procedure wrong. But then Al finally felt
like he could lift his eyelids, and when he did what he
saw blew his mind.

He was moving forward through a tunnel which
was made of swirling colors. As if someone had taken
every color of paint and thrown a bucket of it into a
swirling wall that remained ever changing. More
alarmingly, Alfred could see himself running through
the tunnel of liquid colors. But this did not concern
him, for he felt absolutely amazing. It was as if every
sensor in his brain, every nerve throughout his entire
body was told, "Hey relax. Feel good."

If it were possible to be concerned about anything
while in this state, for Alfred Moreno it would
probably be wondering why there was a gigantic wolf,
with a pelt of shimmering gold, running alongside his
own body he was watching. For the longest time, he
just stared at the wolf and thought about how damn
cool it was. Then he decided to ask some questions.

"Hey wolf, what uh, what's going on here- am I
going to see Gosia?"

"Well of course you are sir!" the Wolf turned and looked at Alfred running beside him.

"*Henry*, is that you?" Al was in disbelief, but the voice, it must be.

"Yes sir! Oh my, I hope I haven't frightened you with my appearance. You see sir, this is how I see myself most of the time. And this place we are in, this is where I always am, in some form or another- ever since you put Gosia's Crystal in me. Now both of us are essentially within the crystal, but at no particular place in time. And since Gosia is a god and gods are in all things, I believe we can now meet with him."

"I gotta say Henry I really only understood maybe a third of what you just said- but you are a lot cooler as a wolf. Although I really think you should change your voice to something a little more intimidating."

The wolf looked Alfred up and down, and then in what sounded like the voice of a champion gladiator announced, "How about *THIS* ?"

If Alfred thought he had eyes right now and wasn't in some sort of strange out of body metaphysical state, he probably would've wiped a tear. He'd never dreamed Henry could be so cool. Up ahead it looked like the path continued both straight and to the left. A loud and commanding voice could be heard coming from the path that was quickly approaching on the left side.

"Yes! China for the win in table tennis! HA HA HA, fifty more years Gardtrof! HAHA!" the voice boomed.

"Climb on my back Alfred, whatever is ahead we will face it together. I have quite an array of powers in this dimension." Henry announced, still in gladiator voice.

Alfred watched as his body seemed to automatically follow Henry's instructions, and climbed to sit on the wolf. Suddenly Alfred snapped back into his own body and was aware of all of his senses. Henry changed his steps so that they veered to the path on the left.

"There is very little data on this subject Alfred, however from what I've found in the records of the Rift Society it seems that a human cannot pass through the gateway to the realm of a god in a physical state. Your spirit is allowed to flow, and it is theorized you can see and communicate through your third eye- that's likely what you were experiencing before. However, even though I am alive, I am not human. I can exist in this place both physically and spiritually. When you climbed onto my back, we became as one- and so long as we are in contact here you will be the same as you would be anywhere else. I think once we pass through the portal you should be fine. So just stay on my back for now."

Alfred did nothing, but instead nodded and patted his hand on Henry's side. For once he was truly thankful beyond words for the A.I. He had been priceless on this journey since escaping the cruise, and Al was starting to think of him more as a friend than just a computer program. He was alive, after all.

Suddenly the colors stopped splashing all around them and they slowed down as a room took shape. Walls came out of the colors, they were white but lit up by blue and red lights in the ceiling. In one corner there was a very extravagant piano. In the middle of the room was a bright yellow futon. On it sat a larger than normal raven, who they soon discovered to be the owner of the booming voice. On a lime green lazy chair next to the futon sat an owl, with four eyes on its head. Two sets of two- each with a different pair of glasses on.

The owl spoke up, not paying any attention to the visitors, "Whatever Dorsen. Double or nothing on javelin!"

"HAHA! So be it, you'll end up owing me a hundred years of your knowledge next!" the raven, Dorsen, announced in an intimidating voice.

"Are you guys betting on the Olympics?" Alfred spoke up out of the blue.

"Yes. Care to get in on the action? What do you have to offer? That wolf is quite intriguing." the Raven interrogated.

"What year is that? Is that Rome, 1960?" Alfred said, looking at the large television screen they were all watching with keen interest.

The owl fumbled around and lifted the remote up somehow with its wing. Then, lowering its beak, it pecked at a button. The guide on the television broadcast showed up, clarifying that it was in fact the 1960 Rome Olympics.

"Yes, that is correct." the owl, who spoke in a low soft voice answered. He then returned the monitor back to the video.

"Well I'm not really interested in betting my awesome golden wolf with incredible powers here on a simple game like javelin." Alfred complained.

"Oh is that so? You'd rather bet on a different Summer Olympic event? Take your pick stranger, and announce the terms."

"Canoeing. If my pick wins you tell me how to get to Gosia. I'm a friend of his, but I've never met him in his own realm- only in the dimension I call home. If your pick wins, you get to take my wolf forever."

Henry spoke up in his masculine voice, "Sir, are you sure about this?"

"Don't worry Henry, I'm a very lucky guy."

Henry whimpered a bit but the Owl, known as Gardtrof, spoke up, "Wow, impressive voice. But what else makes this wolf a worthy trade? You mentioned powers?"

"Uh yeah, Henry show them your um- your powers."

"Of course sir."

The wolf turned, Al still on his back, and looked directly at the elegant piano in the corner. He opened his mouth, exposing lines of golden fanged teeth. Then he made a very strange noise and blasted a beam of golden light at the piano. It immediately transformed into Gardtrof, and to Alfred and everyone else's amazement, the piano was now awkwardly placed in the lazy chair that the owl had been sitting in.

"Woah what a trip! We need this wolf Dorsen."

"Okay, the wolf is cool enough. You have a deal." Dorsen announced, doing something to the remote which made it fast forward in time to the canoeing event.

"We'll pick first." the owl announced.

The birds shuffled over close to one another and spoke in hushed tones. Then Dorsen looked at Alfred and announced, "We pick USA."

"I was actually going to pick Russia, so this works out. Let's watch boys." Alfred responded, directing Henry to walk over and get a better view of the television.

"Russia?" the owl said, confused.

"You said he'd want to pick USA, you fool! You're supposed to be smart!" Dorsen boomed at the owl.

"Well...well...I um…" the owl was backing up away from Dorsen, blinking all four of his eyes very quickly out of panic.

"Hey now, no take backs. You guys wouldn't try to cheat a mere human, when you two are such powerful entities would ya? Be sad if you had to cheat just to beat me." Alfred spoke thoughtfully.

"No. We do not need to cheat to win this bet. Let us watch." Dorsen had calmed down, and went to sit on the couch. Gardtrof sat down a little further away from him.

Everyone watched the black and white screen and listened closely to the commentator as the event began.

"What an extraordinary day we have here for the canoeing finals. The race is off and everyone seems to be sticking close together. Germany is ahead by just one length." the commentator spoke in Italian, but Al realized he could understand him perfectly.

The race went on for a bit and towards the end both USA and Russia had pulled ahead from the other teams. The finish line was fast approaching. There were no rapids and the water followed a path straight ahead.

"And it looks like USA is going to win this one! They've just got the final stretch to go. Russia looks worn out, I'm not sure they have any chance of getting back in the lead."

"HAHA suckers, go ahead and get off our wolf." Dorsen hollered.

"Wait." Al smiled and pointed at the screen, which Dorsen turned back to face and watched.

It certainly looked like USA was about to win, they just had a few more lengths to go and Russia was about two canoe-lengths behind them. Then the oddest thing happened, the USA team's canoe suddenly rolled over- spilling all of the passengers into the water. It looked like there was a flash of light underwater for a moment as well. Al listened as the announcer came on:

"OH! USA has tipped their canoe, and there goes Russia! THERE THEY GO! AND IT'S RUSSIA FOR THE WIN!"

"Oh my…" said Gardtrof quietly.

Surprisingly, the raven did not appear angry or worked up. If anything at all it seemed impressed that a human had managed to defeat him- a spiritual being. When he finally spoke, he looked Alfred in the eyes with a new respect.

"You are wise Alfred Moreno. And it seems luck does indeed follow you. Although I know it was not luck that won you this game. I saw the flash of light, you must've had a Rift Society mission some time ago that took you to that very event. And you changed the outcome of that race long ago in protection of something in the Universe. In turn it helped you out today. How interesting." Dorsen seemed to get lost in thought for a moment.

"That's why I was confident in any bet I placed after I confirmed it was the 1960 Olympics. I had an assignment to go there and make it so that Russia won more medals. By doing so we strengthened national morale, and helped keep the Cold War at bay during those years. It was me who flipped that canoe." Alfred explained.

"There is something about you. You have great destinies to fulfill. I will of course hold up my end of the bet, but if you don't mind I'd like to see if I couldn't help you out a little more."

Alfred looked at the raven curiously as he answered, "Sure! I'll take all the help I can get."

"Gardtrof, come here." Dorsen called to his companion who flew over beside them. "What gifts of knowledge can you provide this Resolver with?"

Gardtrof seemed to think for a moment, then answered, "My gift to you is this: I shall reveal to you the one thing you need to know the most. Other than how to get to Gosia, because Dorsen has already agreed to tell you that. In addition to this, you and your wolf are always welcome in my library."

"Wow, thank you Gardtrof." Al bowed his head to the owl, then asked, "What library is that?"

Gardtrof looked surprised that the human didn't know, but he answered back in a kind tone.

"Why the Great Library of Alexandria of course. Few can go there anymore, but if you ever find yourself requiring knowledge, you are welcome."

"Thank you. So what is it that I need to know the most?"

The owl looked at Al, studying him for a moment.

"The Crystal of Gosia. Although it has many powers, the one which you must be made aware of is its power of duplication."

"But why would I need to know that?" Al looked confused. He was about to return the crystal to Gosia as soon as they told him where he was.

"That is unclear for now. Only the One knows all the answers. Not even Dorsen, Gosia, or I know everything. Now- off to see the god you go!"

Alfred looked to Dorsen who was picking up the t.v. remote. He clicked something on it that made the channel change to an incredibly clear image of a long dirt path leading to a cottage by the sea. The only way one could tell it wasn't a still picture was by the trees moving just slightly in a gentle breeze.

"Step inside and you will be in Gosia's realm. I'm sure he'll be glad to see you. Perhaps our paths will cross again Alfred Moreno. Until then or until never- I wish you well." Dorsen bellowed.

Henry walked up to the large television screen and Alfred reached out his hand and put the tips of his finger against it. To his surprise they went right through it, and he felt the gentle breeze against his fingers.

"So long wolf! So long Alfred!" Gardtrof called to them.

Alfred gave the two birds one last grin, and then urged Henry to go forward into the screen. Henry steadied himself for a moment and then leaped into the television. Suddenly they were on the dirt path, feeling the gentle sunshine and soft breeze. Alfred turned his head to look behind him, expecting to see the blue and red lit room he had been in before. But the path just stretched on down some rolling hills as far as he could see. It looked like there were mountains way off in the distance.

"Alfred. I have sensed that you don't need to be in physical contact with me in this place." Henry spoke in his normal voice, cheerful as ever.

"You sure?" Al asked.

"Positive."

Alfred swung his legs to one side and let himself fall to the ground. He let his hand off of Henry's back, and sure enough he was still in his body. Al stepped in front of Henry and began to lead the way down the dirt path towards the cottage.

It was white in color with a reddish-orange roof and matching shutters. There were many beautiful flowers arranged in beds near the porch of the cottage, which had a wooden swinging bench on it made of polished mahogany. As they neared the porch Henry stood beside Alfred, who shrugged and knocked on the green front door. They waited several minutes, but no one answered.

"Perhaps we should try the backyard?" Henry suggested.

Alfred nodded and walked around the back side of the cottage, which had a patio leading to the beach and sea within a few dozen yards. There was a dock with a small row boat tied to it. The pair walked down the wooden planks to investigate.

"Maybe he's not here. But then what am I supposed to do? I *have* to get a new sun for Hemphion."

"Alfred, look! Out there on the water!" Henry announced.

Alfred looked out and didn't see anything at first, but then sure enough he noticed a small row boat like the one next to them. It was out quite a ways from the shore. It looked as if there were someone standing in it, but Alfred couldn't make out any details.

"Maybe we can ask him. Give me a hand with this rope." Alfred said to Henry.

The wolf chomped through the rope that held the boat to the dock. Then the two of them scrambled into it and Alfred found a pair of oars sitting in the bottom. He picked them up and began to row out towards the other boat. Although he wasn't exactly sure how things worked in this place, he could feel the heat of the sun beating down on him. He stopped rowing for a moment and took off his jacket. Then he took off the plaid button up shirt under it as well, which had become quite dirty and even ripped in a few places.

"Do you feel hot?" Alfred asked the wolf.

"I do not feel things such as temperature in this place. I feel content." Henry answered.

"Then take care of my jacket for me." and as he said this Alfred took his leather jacket and draped it over the wolf's back.

"You like the jacket then sir? You really do?"

"It grew on me Henry, and so have you. Anyway, I guess I feel more qualified to wear it now."

Henry seemed pleased, but said nothing more. Al continued to row on towards the boat, and by the time they were close enough to see who it was his body was glistening in a coat of sweat. Al was surprised when he saw it was Gosia standing up in the boat.

"Well would you look at that, you finally made it. Hold on a minute Al." Gosia spoke, he had the wizened voice of an older man.

Alfred had seen Gosia a couple times before. One other time he was in the form of this same old man. The first time Alfred had witnessed the god in his genuine form. But it had been too overwhelming so Gosia made himself appear as the old man, who apparently enjoyed fishing- as he was reeling something in when he spoke to Al.

He was tall and wiry in stature, and had long hair braided tightly into two pigtails which fell evenly onto his back. His hair was a fine blonde and he had a thin whitening beard. Overtop of his head he had on a fishing hat, with lures stuck in all around it. He wore a soft pink long sleeved shirt and light brown pants with his bare feet tucked into a pair of white sandals.

Alfred and Henry watched as the old man reeled in his line. Whatever was on the other end must have been a decent size. Alfred could see that Gosia's image was quite muscular for the age he had chosen, for the old man's muscles flexed through his shirt as he fought to reel in his catch.

"There she is! What a beauty!" he lifted up a very flat but large red fish, his hand holding it by the mouth.

"Nice catch old man." Alfred said to the god.

"So, I believe you've brought me something Rift Resolver?" Gosia asked, his voice becoming serious as he sat down in his boat.

Alfred tossed a small anchor that was in his own boat into the water so it wouldn't float away as they talked.

"Yes, I have the crystal." Alfred replied, preparing himself to be bold enough to ask the god for a favor.

"Well, toss it over here. Where is it?" the old man laughed a little as he spoke.

Alfred realized for the first time he actually had no idea where the crystal was. He thought he was inside it, but maybe not anymore. He fumbled his hands into his pants pocket and to his relief they found something small and hard. It seemed to gleem brighter than ever before in the dazzling sunlight reflected by the sea. Alfred stared at the crystal sitting flat in his palm for a minute.

"Why do you hesitate Rift Resolver? Was it not foretold to you that you were to return me my crystal, so that horrific events did not end up occurring in the Universe? Few creatures of flesh can use such an artifact, and those that can would likely use it for vile purposes. You have fulfilled all of your responsibilities Alfred Moreno, and you have fully earned my trust. The trust of a god is a valuable thing." Gosia's voice seemed to linger on his last statement, as if warning Alfred to be careful with what he said next.

"I need a favor." Alfred choked out.

"Oh is that so? And what might this favor be?" the god narrowed his eyes.

"The planet Hemphion. It needs a new sun or it'll be destroyed and melted- killing everyone left on it and making the others evacuate never to see their homes again."

"I see." Gosia began, giving Alfred a deep look of understanding before he spoke again, "I do see your motives behind such a request. I admire them. But I'm afraid I can't grant you this favor. It is not the way of the gods to interfere in something as natural as a star dying out. Besides, Hemphion is not under my jurisdiction. If I were to intervene and replace every dying star for every planet that was to be destroyed- I'd completely throw off the balance of the Universe. So as much as I'd like to help you Al, I cannot with this particular request."

Alfred swallowed hard. He had thought this would likely be the god's answer. What he said next however, he didn't realize until he got it out that he had the guts to say it at all.

"Then I guess I'm sorry too. Because I can't give you this crystal until Hemphion gets a new sun. There's someone I owe it too."

"And love is a powerful thing. But I'm afraid I can't simply allow you to leave here with my crystal."

"I hope you understand Gosia. I will return it soon. Henry do something!" as Al finished speaking, he saw something few people in the galaxy had ever seen before. A look of surprise came across the god's face.

Henry opened his mouth wide and blasted a gold beam that completely destroyed half of Gosia's boat.

"Stupid! You are both so stupid! DO YOU KNOW WHO YOU'RE MESSING WITH?" the old man boomed, scrambling to hold onto the half of the boat that still remained afloat.

Meanwhile, Alfred was paddling the oars as fast as he possibly could back toward the cottage.

"I hate to do this to you Al, but I need that crystal back!" yelled the old man to the escaping boat.

Gosia picked up the fish he had caught earlier, which was still flopping around on the half of the boat that wasn't destroyed. He raised it above his head with both arms and energy started filling into the fish, making it glow bright red. Gosia then threw the fish in Alfred's direction. The old man pulled his shirt off and dove into the same spot, disappearing beneath the surface of the water.

"You are crazy sir. Why are we angering the god we're supposed to be helping?" Henry questioned, sounding panicked.

"Because I can't. Let. Marcie. Down." Alfred spoke through his intense paddling.

"Um sir. Don't look now, but there's a shirtless old man riding on the back of a giant red sea monster chasing after us."

Ignoring Henry's advice, Alfred turned and looked behind him. The sea churned around them as a colossal red serpent rose in and out of the water. Holding onto one of its incredibly long whiskers from each side of its face was a shirtless Gosia. With these, he directed the beast as if it were a horse and he held the reins.

"Give me back my damn crystal, Moreno! Before I have ol' Red here blast you a new one!" the god's voice boomed at Alfred's boat.

Alfred turned and looked at Henry, "Think you can match him? I just need you to buy us some time so I can reopen the portal and we can get out of here."

"I'll see what I can do sir!" Henry chirped back quickly.

The gold wolf jumped into the water that surrounded the boat. Alfred continued to furiously row, trying to stay ahead of the giant monster that was quickly gaining on him. In the water behind him Henry swam out until he was at the midway point between the boat and Gosia.

Henry's body began to glow as he dived under the water. Alfred looked back a few moments later, and saw no sign of the A.I. Damn it, he thought, where is he? Gosia's serpent was about to reach where Henry had disappeared.

Just then, an enormously bright gold light flashed in the depths of the sea- all the way up through the water. Gosia's monster was just crossing over the light when a magnificent beast, very similar to the red one- rushed up and broke the surface. It was Henry, who had taken the form of a massive golden sea dragon. Henry grabbed the red serpent's neck in his rows of jagged sharp teeth.

Gosia was shaken off and began to slide down the length of his beast, but was able to get a grip on a scale and began to make his way back up. The red beast somehow managed to break free from Henry's grasp. Henry rose into the air, beating a scaly pair of large golden wings. Alfred watched as Henry the dragon opened his jaws and blasted a golden beam of energy into the side of the red serpent. Alfred couldn't believe his eyes. There was a massive gaping hole, all the way through Gosia's serpent. And better yet, Gosia had slid off during the damage and was now swimming in the water next to it. The red creature groaned in pain.

"You bastards! You shot a hole through ol' Red!" Gosia yelled out to Alfred, who had started rowing away.

"Come on Henry, give me a lift to the shore!" Al yelled to the flying A.I.

The dragon swooped down and gently clutched Al in his claws, carrying him to the shore. When he set him down, Henry shrunk back down into the wolf he had been before.

"Great shot by the way! Get ready to go!" Al praised.

Taking the crystal out of his pocket and his Rift Blade from his belt, Al prepared to open the portal back to his dimension. Gosia had swam closer and was approaching the beach with unnatural speed.

"You lowered my sea monster's self-esteem Moreno! And you owe me my crystal!" the old man yelled as he reached the sand and began to run toward the pair.

"Jump in Henry!" yelled Al as he slammed his blade into the center of the crystal which sat on the sand. This time Al could see the portal open as if he had cut a rift in time, and in front of him was the swirling circle that led into the colorful tunnel. Al climbed quickly onto Henry's back, who immediately leaped into the portal. Just before it closed behind them, Alfred yelled back to the god.

"I'll bring it back I promi-" and then the portal closed.

Gosia sat down on the beach, shaking his head for a moment before succumbing to a chuckle.

"Sometimes it's better to see how these things play out than to intervene. I would be surprised after all, if Moreno could find a way to use my crystal to create a new sun. HA HA HA!" the old man laughed to himself as if the idea was ridiculous.

Just then the red sea monster swam up, and Gosia approached it as it sat near the rolling tide that washed repeatedly onto the shore.

"I am sorry master. I have failed you." the red serpent slithered to the god in an ancient tongue.

"It's okay my friend. Come now, let us fix that hole!" Gosia led the way back up to his cottage with the giant serpent slithering up the beach after him.

7 NOT QUITE A BLACK-TIE AFFAIR

Alfred flew back out of the portal, landing on the ground roughly. Getting his bearings, he realized he was once again fully clothed. And other than what would likely turn out to be a decent sized bruise tomorrow, he was unscathed. Not a single bead of sweat was on his forehead that had been covered just moments before. But something *was* different- the whole room was shaking. His attention snapped back to the Rift Sanctum as he got up and Marcie yelled.

"Alfred, you're back already? Something's happening!"

"What do you mean already? And why's the whole place shaking?" Alfred asked, confused.

"I don't know, you'd only been gone a minute or so and then the floor started shaking beneath my feet, and then you came flying out of nowhere onto the ground! Did you see Gosia? Did he create a new sun for Hemphion?" Marcie asked, her face pleading for a yes.

Alfred looked away for a moment and then began to talk out loud to himself.

"Gosia...crystal. Where's the crystal?" his voice grew louder at the end with worry.

Turning around, he was relieved to see it sitting on the table. He grabbed it quickly and went to put it in his inner jacket pocket, but felt something already inside. He reached his hand in and pulled out the golden egg.

"Hello sir! Glad to see we made it back through alright. Oh my, why is this room so unstable? You know they should have made this place much more structurally sound, there's always meteor showers passing through this part of the Universe."

"Looks like Henry's back to being lame." Alfred announced, tucking the crystal into his other pocket.

"Whaaa... what's going on? Somebody vacuuming?" a concussed Aaron Flux asked as he blinked his eyes open, laying on the floor.

"No, nobody's vacuuming moron. Alfred, why do you still have Gosia's Crystal?" Marcie narrowed her eyes as she spoke.

"Come on, we need to get upstairs and quick. I'll fill you in later." he answered, beginning to run back up the stairs to the roller-rink.

Marcie and a dazed Aaron Flux stumbled up after him. Alfred reached the top and pushed a button, opening the secret door in the rink floor. He stepped out into chaos. Humans and aliens and everything in between were running for the doors, trampling over each other in an attempt to get out. Alfred covered his face with his arms as something blasted into the ceiling, shaking the entire building and causing rubble to fall all over the floor around him and his companions.

"Oh, shit." Flux announced blatantly- to be fair it was about all one could say.

Above them a giant hole had been broken in the ceiling. Riding down from the roof were ten different men, each wearing a tuxedo of a different color.

Alfred looked to Marcie, "Friends of yours?"

"They're an elite group of Sham-Bon's men. His personal protectors and body-guards. If they're here, so is he." she looked concerned.

"Looks like the big scary king is staying in his spaceship. Come on, we've got to hold this place down, it means everything to Papari and Jenni." Al turned to Aaron, "Flux, you okay to fight?"

"I don't know what day of the week it is. But hey, since when does any Rift Resolver? Let's do it Moreno. You too red armor chick- um what was your name again?" Flux looked at Marcie.

Marcie simply rolled her eyes. They didn't have time to talk any longer, Sham-Bon's men were now landing on the rink. They had ridden down on collapsible hoverboards. Half of them remained in the air, each looked to be armed with an energy gun. Alfred looked like he was about to charge at them, but Marcie grabbed him by the shoulder.

"Alfred, you don't have on any shoes. The roller-blades remember, we took them off after your little finale?"

"Right. Shoes. And how is it that I'm the only one not wearing shoes?"

Henry chirped gleefully from inside Al's jacket, "I don't have on any shoes either Alfred!"

A man in a neon green tuxedo, armed with a fully automatic energy rifle, approached them.

"Haha, get a load of this guy! The famous Al Moreno, barefoot. What, is the Rift Society not paying you losers enough to afford shoes?" the man laughed along with several of his associates.

Underneath the neon tuxedo the man wore a white undershirt and a tie that matched his jacket. He had short blonde hair that was slicked back. Alfred noticed that all of Sham-Bon's men looked vaguely similar.

"Yeah yeah yeah. Laugh it up boys, what'd you all go shoot up a neon sign store before this?" Alfred laughed to himself as he spoke.

The Huck men stopped laughing, except one who was still up in the air on his hoverboard.

"This guy's pretty funny- neon sign store!"

The man in front of Alfred began to frown, turning around he yelled up to the man in a violet suit.

"Shut it Violet. Don't make me come up there."

"I take it your name's Green then? Or is it Leprechaun?" Alfred taunted.

"Enough of this! Give us Gosia's Crystal now."

"As if." Al replied.

"Have it your way. What a shame we have to trash such a wonderful little roller-rink."

Green pulled his gun so that it aimed right at Alfred's chest. Marcie and Flux tensed beside him.

ZING!

Alfred opened his eyes wide with shock as an energy rifle round flew from the right, traveling through the air faster than sound until it stopped in the middle of Green's head. The man in the tuxedo dropped to the floor, instantly dead. Alfred turned to see where the shot had come from.

Up on a balcony to the right was an old woman. In her hands was a long sniper rifle, still smoking at the barrel from the powerful energy round that had just been blasted out of it. She wore a nice white dress and two golden hoop earrings in each ear. Her face was wrinkled to where one could tell she was quite old, but her eyes flared with fire. Her gray hair was neatly pulled into a bun on the top of her head. Two fine red wooden sticks stuck in her hair.

"Nobody's trashing this Roller-Rink. You've already destroyed my ceiling! And do you realize how long it's going to take to wax that floor? A hell of a lot longer now that Leprechaun boy is bleeding all over it!" the old woman yelled out to the Huck men.

"Jenni! Looks like you haven't missed a beat. Thanks for that by the way." Alfred called up to her.

"Anything for you Al, now come on- let's get these bastards out of here!" she yelled back.

"You guys hold them off while I get a gun!" Alfred instructed his companions as he ran towards the counter near the entrance.

By now most of the rollerbladers and crowd had made it safely out of the doors and were all taking off in spaceships in the parking lot.

"Hey, they killed Green! The boss isn't gonna be happy- get 'em!" a man called Blue directed the other men.

Al zig-zagged all the way across the rink floor, bullets beginning to pepper the ground around him. He could see Papari up ahead ducking under the counter and every few seconds popping up to unload a clip from an assault rifle.

"Hey old man, you got my shoes and an extra gun?" Al yelled to him as he ran.

Papari smirked and grabbed Al's shoes, throwing them over the counter. There was something big and metal in one of them- it was an energy revolver.

Alfred was about to reach it when someone landed right in front of him. It was a man in a yellow suit. He looked to be unarmed.

"Just a second there slick. You're not going anywhere." Yellow stated.

"Oh yeah? And who's going to stop me? You, Banana man?"

"Enough talk." the man replied, reaching his arms behind his head and pulling out two longswords.

Alfred looked around quickly, Marcie was tied up with a guy in red. Flux was firing his own energy revolver at two of the guys up on the hoverboards. Papari was busy keeping Jenni covered while she aimed down at a man in orange. Al had no choice but to take this guy on himself.

Reaching to his waist he grabbed and flicked open his Rift Blade. The man with the swords paused for a moment to laugh.

"That's not much of a sword."

"You must not know much about Rift Resolvers, eh Banana man?"

"All I know is my boss wants that crystal and you have it. Therefor, you die." he swung one of the blades out, but Alfred met it quickly with his knife.

They went on like this for a couple of minutes, with Yellow on the offensive and Al simply trying to block all of his attacks.

Sling!

Alfred grimaced as the edge of one of Yellow's blades sliced into his shoulder.

"You're not bad, but how long can you keep this up?" Yellow asked.

"You're right, probably not much longer. So let's make this quick!" Al yelled as he jumped back from the man, and reached into his jacket pocket pulling out Henry.

Al threw Henry on the ground beside Yellow, who dove away from the golden egg.

"HAHA what're you doing on the ground over there?" Alfred chuckled, raising up his Rift Blade in his right hand.

"Nice trick. I thought it was a grenade, but it didn't get you anywhere." Yellow sneered, beginning to get to his feet.

"It got me some distance for a nice throw, eh Banana? Or should I call you Banana Split now?" Alfred laughed at his own cheesy joke.

"What're you talk- ugh!" the man choked in pain as Alfred pulled back his arm and threw the blade in one swift motion, sticking it in Yellow's chest.

Alfred watched as a rift opened in the middle of the man, sucking his body into the portal from the inside out.

"Ouch, I bet that hurt!" Al said as he picked up his knife off the ground, and ran to his shoes and gun.

Quickly he slid his feet into them and picked up the energy revolver. Looking behind the counter, he saw a man in blue choking Papari around the throat with both hands. Alfred closed his left eye, and took aim with his revolver.

CRACK

The bullet exploded powerfully out of the revolver, hitting Blue right in the side of the head. His hands slowly released the old man who was coughing as he tried to regain his breath. Alfred ran the rest of the way to him.

"Thanks kid!" Papari said to Al.

"No problem! Now come on, let's take care of the rest of these guys."

They both took cover below the counter and began firing rounds at what was left of the Huck men. Soon enough there was just one more remaining, the man wearing the Violet suit that had been laughing before. He was firing nonstop rounds at Marcie. She ducked, dove, and danced all over the floor, making sure her head wasn't hit. Other than that she simply let the bullets hit against her armor, it would take more than energy rounds to pierce through the rare metal.

Alfred laughed when he saw Violet continuing to pull the trigger but no more bullets were coming out. He was out of ammo. Marcie stopped her dodging and stood up straight. She touched something on her arm that opened a small case, from which she pulled out a throwing star.

"Woah, red-armor chick has some cool weapons! What, are you like a ninja or something?" Flux asked while catching his breath.

Marcie turned at him and glared, "How do you not know my name!"

"Um Mary? Margret?" Flux offered.

Marcie rolled her eyes and turned back to Violet, who had an odd look on his face.

"Hey lady, do I know you or something?" Violet asked, not seeming to realize he was in a very bad position.

"No." Marcie replied, a serious look in her eye.

"Wait a second, yes I do, you worked for- UGH!" the man grimaced as Marcie stuck the throwing star into his arm.

"Haha look at that, she just got my arm!" Violet seemed okay with this and reached his hand down as if to pull it out.

But just as he was about to pull it out, Alfred noticed Marcie had an amused look on her face. Everyone in the rink watched as the star started to spin faster and faster as it moved up Violet's arm, cutting deep and sending blood flying everywhere. Violet screamed in pain as the star went up to his shoulder, then down his chest and finally dug deep into where his heart was before finally coming to a halt. The man dropped dead on the floor, essentially a giant pile of scraps.

"Wow. That's some throwing star you got there Marce." Alfred said as he, Papari, and Jenni made their way over to her and Flux.

"First of all, don't call me Marce. Second, that's a vein-chaser. Stick it in an enemy and it will find the nearest vein and trace it back to your heart, cutting the whole way." she explained.

"How...lovely." Flux said awkwardly.

"Sorry about all the blood Jenni." Marcie said to the old woman, who held hands with Papari.

"Oh it's fine dear. I'm glad to see Al has someone like you watching out for him. I'm angrier about that big hole in my ceiling, but we'll get it fixed up soon enough." she replied, and Marcie looked embarrassed for a moment.

"Um excuse me everyone, but there is something coming through the hole right now." Henry announced.

Al looked up at the sound of Henry's voice. Sure enough, a small spacecraft was hovering just outside of the hole. A balcony unfolded from the door of the ship, which then slid open. A large man wearing a black tuxedo stepped out. On his tux there was a blue rose pinned. He was quite tall and sturdy in stature. It was hard to make out too much of the details of his face, but Al noticed he had a scar stretching across his left cheek. He had a medium-length beard as well, that made him seem even more intimidating. The man stood on the balcony for a moment clapping his hands slowly before laughing a little.

"Well, well. Looks like the legends are true about you Alfred Moreno. Took out my whole little well-dressed squad, and managed to steal away my prized assassin too." the man looked only at Al, ignoring Marcie and the rest of them.

"I take it you're Sham-Bon then?" Al asked, meeting his gaze all the way.

"That's right. You keep your little crystal for now, but I am in need of it. And I will have it." Sham-Bon spoke as if it were certain.

"Not while I'm alive. What do you want it for anyway?" Al asked.

"Oh, a variety of things I suppose. I was *going* to use it to save Hemphion of course. But seeing as how the very child I raised has decided to turn traitor, perhaps I'll use it to destroy her village instead."

"You'll never destroy us and you'll never get the crystal!" Marcie yelled furiously up at her old boss, her emotions getting the best of her.

Alfred turned to his right, his eyes opening wide as he noticed Jenni was aiming down at Sham-Bon with her energy rifle.

"You wrecked my Roller-Rink, scum!" she growled as she pulled the trigger.

The bullet smacked dead-on into Sham-Bon's head, which flung backward in an unnatural way after being hit by the bullet. But his solid body didn't drop, it remained standing upright. Alfred watched in surprise as the king's head slowly raised back up from where his neck was bent backwards until he was perfectly fine. Even the bullet hole had sealed itself back up.

"It's going to take a lot more than that to kill me. I *will* have that crystal Moreno." the head of the Huck Family declared as he stepped back inside of the small spacecraft.

The door collapsed shut behind him and whoever was piloting the ship took off into space. Everyone turned to Al once Sham-Bon's ship had left.

"Well what're you looking at me for? We've got some work to do and I need to figure out how to use Gosia's Crystal to create a new sun. I think I may know a way to do it, but I need some more information. Luckily I've got about ten years left to work it out before the sun explodes." Alfred sounded confident- as if he had taken Sham-Bon's declaration as a personal challenge not to let him get his hands on the crystal.

"Not quite...I hate to be the bearer of bad news here, but that's what that report on the news was about that you turned off. You see, during your trip here four years have gone by on the planet Hemphion. So it's got approximately six years left until uh... well you know." Flux gulped as he finished speaking.

"Alright, six years- I can still do this!" Al announced, not discouraged in the slightest.

"No Al, you're not realizing the bigger problem that raises." Marcie began, a look of concern growing in her eyes. "By the time we travel to Hemphion to try and save it, it might be too late."

Alfred did not look nearly as confident now. He looked as if he wanted to say something but couldn't think of what he could possibly do if it would already be too late by the time they got there.

"Wait! I have just performed the calculations and if we leave for Hemphion in the next hour there will still be about three days remaining until the sun explodes. Hemphion's surface might be a little warmer than usual- but it will be liveable all the way up until eight minutes after the sun explodes. That's how long it will take the force of the explosion to travel to the planet. Oddly enough, I retrieved most of the information regarding Hemphion's sun from the royal Huck Family's database." Henry spoke up and explained.

The team looked around at each other. It was hard to be optimistic with only three days to learn how to create a new sun. Alfred looked down for a moment, seemingly disheartened by what everyone was beginning to think. Then he looked up and spoke.

"Three days and eight minutes. If we leave as soon as possible that gives us just a little more time. Hey old man," he turned to Papari, "How's about lending me a ship?"

Papari looked surprised for a moment, then a smile came over his face.

"That's the Al I know- you got it buddy." The man exchanged a look with his wife- there was no mistaking the pride they had in the young man they adopted.

"You can't be serious Alfred! This is beyond what I can ask of you, you'll be risking your life for a planet that you have no attachment to whatsoever. If we fly to Hemphion there won't be time to get far enough away to escape the blast of the sun. It's suicide." Marcie spoke fiercely as if she couldn't be convinced to let Alfred take on the responsibility.

"It's not suicide if he pulls it off." Flux spoke up, a grin on his face. Marcie looked at him in surprise as he continued, "You're forgetting one important detail here red- I mean Marcie. You've got Al Moreno on your side. And me too. Besides, worst case scenario we open a couple rifts and get the hell out of there!"

"Don't forget about me!" Henry piped up excitedly.

Alfred nodded to Aaron, showing he was thankful for his faith and support.

"It's settled then. We're leaving for Hemphion as soon as possible. Aaron, let's give Papari a hand getting the ship ready." Alfred instructed.

The three men (with Al carrying Henry in his pocket) headed to the parking area behind the building. Marcie remained standing where she was until she felt a wrinkled but firm hand grasp her shoulder.

"For anyone else that never lived on Hemphion, it might seem foolish to risk their life to save a planet they have never been to or know nothing about. But for Alfred, I'm afraid everything in the Universe is valuable. He swore his life to guarding it- and nothing will change his mind if he thinks he can help save one of its planets." Jenni explained.

Marcie's face changed to a soft smile as she replied, "He really is something isn't he?"

"We sure think so! Now come on, let's see if we can give those boys a hand getting the ship ready."

And with that the old sharpshooter and the young assassin headed after their friends.

8 JASHI

"Alright everyone, strap in! We're about to go to hyper speed and you don't want to be standing up when I tell Henry to get this puppy blasting off into space!" Al appeared to be back in high spirits as he spoke to Flux and Marcie.

They had said their goodbyes to Jenni and Papari, who had already begun repairing the damages done by Sham-Bon's men.

The three of them strapped into their seats while Henry configured himself to set the ship at high speed.

"Hello ladies and gentlemen! Welcome to this wonderful flight to Hemphion today. There will be no refreshments during the duration of this trip. The flight will take an estimated thirty minutes. And now as we are about to enter high speed, you should feel a slight bump and then will be able to enjoy the rest of the trip strapped into your seat." as Henry finished speaking the spacecraft leapt forward at insane speeds toward the planet Hemphion.

After a few moments Flux had fallen asleep in his chair, and Marcie turned to talk to Al.

"Do you know how you're going to do it?" she asked anxiously.

"I'll be honest- not exactly. I know the key lies in something to do with duplication. A spiritual entity told me that Gosia's Crystal has that power. So if I can find a way to make a copy of a healthy sun, I should be able to replace the one that is set to explode."

"But...even if you *could* somehow figure out a way to do all of that- won't Hemphion's current sun just blow up into the new one you create?" Marcie looked doubtful.

"One step at a time. I'm going to give this everything I've got, okay? So just bear with me and try to help as much as you can." Alfred tried to reassure her.

"Well, I don't know how much help this will end up being but there's a group of people I want you to talk to when we get to Hemphion."

"Who are they?" Al questioned.

"A community of people known as the Gazers. Many will have likely begun to doubt their wisdom by the time we arrive. But my mother told me when I was little that her parents had been Gazers before they passed away- and that they knew all sorts of secrets about Hemphion. They might know something that can help."

"Hmm." Alfred thought for a moment before speaking back up. "Sounds like a cult."

"Look, like I said they're a little weird- but just listen to anything they might have to offer, I think it could help."

"Alright alright, enough nagging. I'll give the mystical Gazers a chance to speak their minds. If they've got any left..." Al said the last part under his breath.

The two fell silent and the rest of the trip went by fairly quickly. Alfred was studying his Rift Blade when Henry broke the silence- waking Flux in the process.

"We will now be returning to moderate speeds and will land on the planet Hemphion in a few minutes."

"*Yaaaawn*. So what'd I miss?" Flux stretched in his chair, blinking in the white light of the spacecraft's interior.

"We're about to land, come on." Al replied.

They could feel the ship shake as the propulsors slowly decreased their power output. Alfred led the way down into the exit bay and out of the hatch. Henry had landed the vehicle in a medium-sized clearing surrounded by dense trees with full heads of orange-red leaves.

"Uh...Marcie? I thought we were going to start by going to your house. This looks more like a forest." Flux arrogantly pointed out.

"We are, but there wouldn't have been anywhere closer where we could've landed the ship. Follow me, both of you, so you don't get hurt."

"Did she say get hurt?" Flux gulped and turned to Al, who simply shrugged and began to follow after Marcie.

She led the way through the trees as if there were a path under her feet, but not one that Alfred could seem to make out. After a while the brush surrounding them began to grow dense and in the way. Marcie slid a long machete-like blade out of the end of her armor. She sliced as much as she could to make room for the three of them to get through.

"Is it much farther forest-lady?" Aaron called ahead, his shoulders leaned down and he was dragging his feet.

"Not too much, but we can take a short break here." Marcie replied, slowing up.

"Fine...by...me." Flux wheezed, sitting down on the long tendril-like grass beneath him.

Alfred stood for a moment, looking around at the forest that seemed to surround them for miles on end. He looked to the sky and found himself gazing at the sun for a moment. There didn't appear to be anything wrong with it. But Alfred didn't doubt that in three days' time it would explode- and it would be his fault if it did.

Suddenly a flash of movement caught his eye in the heights of a far-off tree. He directed his attention to it and sure enough it looked like there was a figure peering out from the thickness of the leaves.

"Hey guys I think there's some- waaaAAAAAGH!" Alfred found himself being pulled by the legs upward until he swung upside down by a rope looped tight around his ankle.

He watched, upside down, as the flash of movement from the far-off tree zoomed at an incredible speed toward them. Flux was looking at the hanging Alfred with fear and panic in his eyes. Marcie was doing something Al hadn't seen before. She seemed to be laughing hysterically, to the point where she even fell to the ground on her back.

The flash that had zoomed towards them now revealed itself. It was a young boy, with his face painted a bright orange-red just like the leaves in the trees. He had tan skin and long arms for his size. The boy had thrown his knee hard into Flux's back, knocking him to the ground. Alfred watched as the boy then twisted one of Flux's arms around behind his back and held a sharp knife to his throat with his other hand.

By now the blood was beginning to rush to Alfred's head, and he was already too confused by the scene that was playing out before him. He went to grab his Rift Blade from his belt to cut himself down, but just as he reached for it something whizzed passed him and stuck into the tree he hung from, very close to his outstretched limb.

"Do not move if you wish to live." the boy spoke without even looking at Alfred, who allowed his arms to lower back down slowly.

Instead, the boy was staring intently at Marcie who had her legs in the air, still crying out of laughter.

"Marcie, Marcie! Why do you cry, have these men hurt you? Please don't die, I will avenge your death by killing these two if you do."

"Um Marcie, do you want to maybe explain what's going on here?" Alfred asked curiously. Flux appeared to be too nervous to say anything.

Marcie had finally managed to sit up and was able to speak clearly again.

"No Jashi, I'm fine, I'm fine. But wow you sure made these two look stupid!" she let out a few more small laughs.

The boy, Jashi, appeared to be confused. Alfred noticed that his eyes were a bright emerald green, and his skin was a similar tone to Marcie's as well.

"So, you *don't* want me to kill these men?" Jashi asked, loosening his grip a bit on Flux.

"Well Aaron is pretty annoying, but no that's okay Jashi. They're with me actually."

"Oh! I'm sorry Marcie I didn't know. I was just in the forest hunting when I thought I spotted your armor! And then I couldn't believe it was you, and when I realized it was, I thought you might be in danger. So I was trying to save you from these guys."

"Hey sorry to interrupt and all, but could someone please cut me down?" Alfred felt like he was going to pass out soon.

"I've got you sir!" Henry announced.

Out of the pocket of Alfred's jacket a metal material was continuously unfolding, until it reached out and extended upward past Al's face, reaching the rope around his ankle. A pair of small gold scissors unfolded at the very end and snipped the rope, causing Alfred to fall roughly onto the ground.

Alfred rubbed the back of his head where it had hit the ground before slowly getting to his feet.

"Just now Henry? Really?" he flashed the scissors that were slowly lowering back down into his pocket a dirty look.

Meanwhile Jashi had released his hold on Flux. Aaron took a few deep breaths, gave himself a quick check over, and then seemed content that he was alive and unharmed.

"So who's the ninja kid?" he asked as they all came to stand together.

"This is Jashi." Marcie introduced the boy, rubbing her hand on the top of his hair playfully. "He's a boy from my village. He used to spy on me when I would train and eventually I let him join in."

Suddenly Marcie's face furrowed into a frown.

"But Jashi, why do you look as if you're barely any older than you were when I left? You should be a teenager by now."

"Yes...well I suppose I might as well tell you now. You see, my old man's health only got worse after you left. A lot of other people began to get sick too, the scientists say it's something to do with the sun but I don't know. My father, he…" the boy's voice wavered for a moment and he paused before he spoke back up.

"A few years ago he got really bad. They said he only had a few more weeks to live. So he sold our house- sold just about everything we had. And he used the money to get me a cryogenic freeze and be sent off on an outgoing ship, so I wouldn't be here when the sun explodes. But about a year ago the money my father had put down ran out. It had all been used up in supplying my cryogenic container with life material. So they un-froze me and the ship took off without me."

Marcie looked as if she were holding back tears. Flux wept madly.

"Wow, kid. Well it looks like you're tough then- you've made it all this time on your own." Alfred gave the boy a nod, and Jashi smiled.

"But Marcie you've returned! That means you can save Hemphion, right? Come on, the people of the village will be thrilled!"

"Well Jashi...I don't kno-"

Al cut her off, "That's right kid, we're going to get this planet a new sun. Now come on, show us to the village!"

Marcie shot Alfred a thankful look, but he paid it no attention and the three of them followed the boy, who led them through the brush until they came to a dirt path. They followed it for a mile or two until they came to a small compound. There was a wall made of plasti-crete, basically a durable material that many people on poorer planets utilized in building their structures.

They approached a large metal door that was in the center of the wall in front of them. A man stood guard out front with a fully-automatic energy gun.

"Hey Jashi, who are these- is that *you* Marcie?" the man seemed suspicious at first but as soon as he noticed Marcie's armor he grew more and more excited.

"Hey Ardmon! Good to see you. These two are Rift Resolvers, they're here to help." she replied, seeming to perk up a bit at recognizing yet another familiar face.

"Of course, your return! It must mean you've found a way to save our planet! Come on, the others will be thrilled to see you're back."

Ardmon opened the door and led the way through the plasti-crete wall. Alfred followed closely behind and an entire village opened up in front of him. Most of the homes and buildings were made of the same material as the outer-wall, as he had assumed would be the case. Another guard replaced Ardmon's spot outside the main doors and exchanged a similar excited greeting with Marcie as he passed by. Alfred continued to follow close behind their new guide, walking in pace with Jashi.

Ardmon appeared to be a bit on the hefty-side, but Alfred could tell it was mostly made up of muscle. He wore pants and a robe of the same orangish color that seemed to make up most of the nature in the forest around the village. Al noticed a strange rash on the back of the man's neck and wondered if it could be a sign of the disease that the boy said his father and others had died from. Ardmon appeared to be leading them to a building larger than most of the others. It looked to be some sort of house for the needy. As they walked through the doors they came into a courtyard where many older people sat around talking amongst one another. There were children as well, and while Alfred expected them to be playing- they too seemed to be just sitting around.

"Say Jashi, what's the name of your village anyway?" he asked the boy beside him.

"Bratvia. Probably an unfamiliar word to you, it comes from the ancient language of our planet. Few besides the Gazers bother to speak it anymore, but our village's name translates to Land Of The Brave." the boy answered as if he were proud of his village's name.

"Everyone seems so down…" Alfred commented absent-mindedly.

The boy's expression grew fierce, capturing Al's full attention as he spoke.

"Yes, the morale is low. Most have given up hope of being saved and have prepared themselves for the worst. But our village has always continued to stand against the Huck Family, we put our faith in Marcie- because she risked everything by betraying him just for a chance at us being saved. And you're here now, you can help save us. There *is* hope."

Alfred met the boy's eyes and nodded in agreement. He would do everything he could to save the people of Bratvia and the thousands of villages like it all across Hemphion. The group walked through the courtyard turning heads and gaining the attention of the despondent villagers. Their hushed tones picked up in volume and growing enthusiasm as they noticed the newcomers.

They reached the other side and entered through another pair of doors. Ardmon took them into a small lobby where there were several couches and chairs.

"Please sit, I will get Mother Via. She will be glad to see you Marcie. And the rest of you too I suppose!" he added with a hardy chuckle.

Alfred, Marcie, and Aaron took a seat while Jashi walked around a nearby counter that looked to be part of the kitchen. He opened one side of his robe, similar to the one Ardmon wore, and revealed a small furry creature. The boy tossed it onto the counter and began to skin it with a knife. Alfred watched, somewhat repulsed, until Ardmon walked back into the lobby. An elderly woman wearing a long primitive red dress followed closely behind.

"Mother Via!" Marcie sprung up and the old women met her with a warm embrace.

"Marcie, you have returned after all. And it looks as if you've brought some new friends with you as well." the woman smiled at Al and Aaron who stood up as Marcie introduced them.

"Yes, this is Aaron Flux and Alfred Moreno- Rift Resolvers who have come to help us.

The two men shook her feeble hand lightly and then everyone sat back down. Ardmon walked into the kitchen to assist Jashi in preparing his catch.

"A pleasure to meet you both. Now, Marcie- is it true then that you have returned with the Crystal of Gosia?"

"Yes well, we do have the crystal. And we have an idea of how to get Hemphion a new sun- but we aren't exactly sure…" she trailed off, looking to Alfred as if she didn't know what more to say.

"I believe I know a way in which I might be able to duplicate your planet's sun, but I require some guidance on how exactly to do it. Marcie mentioned something about an ancient group known as the Gazers, perhaps you could point us in their direction?"

"The Gazers...it is true they have much wisdom and the people in rural villages across Hemphion once put their faith in the group and the god they worship. But I'm afraid many members of the Gazers have abandoned the god they pray to for understanding and knowledge, and as a result have remained silent for the last few months as the destruction of the sun has grown ever closer. And now… we've only three more days." Mother Via's voice grew softer toward the end, leaning back on the desperation Alfred had felt amongst the other villagers.

"You mean to say they've disbanded completely?!" Marcie exclaimed in shock.

"Well I suppose they still remain living in their temples across the planet, but they send away anyone searching for answers anymore. I'm afraid they're completely useless. They, like many others, have given up all hope."

"I understand it might sound like a worthless effort, but Mother, if you can tell me where the closest temple is I would like to speak to these Gazers- as of now it's the best chance of figuring this out we have." Alfred allowed the urgency to come out in his voice as he pleaded the woman for information.

The old woman seemed to grow lost in thought for a moment and stared blankly around the room. Then she looked back at Alfred, her eyes glimmering with the small light of a newfound hope.

"Very well, if you insist Rift Resolver. I am not one to interfere with the actions of someone who serves to do right in the Universe such as yourself. I will tell you the way."

9 THE GAZERS

The rest of the day went by quite quickly. Mother Via told Alfred where he could find the nearest temple of the Gazers. It was a trip that could be made in a single day if one traveled hard. The first part could be traveled on one of the many dirt roads that connected the rural villages in this area of Hemphion. The second half would have to be journeyed on foot, through the woodlands quite some way.

Alfred had made the decision that he would be going alone, taking only Henry who had the directions memorized. Marcie seemed frustrated that Alfred insisted on the others staying behind.

"You don't know this land- I do!" she had insisted to Al.

"Look Marcie, I know you want to help but Henry has the path in his system and I need you and the others to stay here in case Sham-Bon and his men try anything."

She still seemed angry but eventually accepted that he was probably right. Alfred had spent the remainder of the day resting and talking amongst the villagers of Bratvia. He soon came to learn that although they seemed a cheerless group now, they had indeed once been a village of great warriors. There had been much unrest and misdirected outrage amongst the nearby villages in the past few years. Many had disbanded into groups of anarchists, angry at the world and their god for the seemingly unavoidable fate they all faced. These radical bands had attempted to break through the walls of Bratvia many times- trying to ravage, steal, and kill everything in sight simply because they believed nothing they did had any true consequences anymore. Abandoned by their god, they assumed they would end up in a hell when it was all over regardless of what they now chose to do with their lives. The villagers had fought them off time and time again- keeping their faith only because of Mother Via and the hope that Marcie would return some day with a way to save them.

As Alfred lay in his bed that evening he thought about something Ardmon had told them over dinner.

"The people in rural villages like ours, those that didn't turn to hate and anarchy, have always held more faith in the Gazers than our government. Those who lived in the larger metropolises of the planet evacuated when Parliament declared they had no answer for saving the planet. The rest put their faith in the wisdom of the Gazers who believe that if it is truly meant to be the end for Hemphion, the people of the planet were meant to perish along with it. It must seem foolish to an outsider for people to believe that their existence has truly come to an end...but the Gazers have always been right before."

Alfred lay awake in a room that Mother Via had offered him to stay in that night. There was a skylight above his cot that he watched the light of the moons pour through. There were two of them- Jashi had said they were called Lax and Luts. Alfred looked at them, thinking that they were set to be in just as much peril as the planet they reflected light onto each night.

"I've got to find these Gazers. No matter what. The time of these people is not over yet, not if I can help it." he spoke softly to himself.

As he drifted into a light and troubled sleep that night his last thoughts were not of the people of Bratvia, nor the planet Hemphion, nor even the sun that was fated to explode in two days time. It was the face of a girl- one with long black hair and emerald eyes that drew him in like nothing he had ever experienced before. A girl who had sacrificed her whole life just to try to save her planet and people. Now he would take on that responsibility and sacrifice whatever it took to make things right.

***

Alfred woke early the next morning to the warm rays of the sun pouring in through the skylight. As he got out of bed he thought it strange that a sun so near death looked and felt the same as any other. He showered and dressed quickly in his clothes that one of Mother Via's helpers had kindly washed and left folded by his bedside. His ears perked at the sound of children laughing, so he decided to walk out into the courtyard to investigate.

In the grassy lawn before him he saw something which he did not expect. The same children who had sat around gloomily the night before were now engaged in a game of catch- throwing around a small shiny metal object.

"Put me down! Stop throwing me! I insist you little mongrels put me down at once!" Alfred recognized Henry's voice coming from his device, which was currently being tossed high into the air.

Alfred laughed to himself and approached the children.

"Henry, looks like you've made some new friends!" he called out.

"Alfred! Please, please tell these children to stop throwing me!" Henry pleaded.

"Alright, alright kids. As much as I like to see Henry getting thrown around a bit, I need him back now for a mission."

One of the smaller boys approached him, handing Henry over when he got close.

"Is it true you're a Rift Resolver? And you've come to get us a new sun and save us all?" he asked in awe.

"That's right kid, I'll see you all back here in a day's time and Hemphion will be just fine!" Alfred replied, invoking small jumps and cheers amongst the children.

Alfred headed back into the lobby that they had sat around talking in the night before. Aaron, Marcie, and Ardmon stood waiting for him. Flux approached him first, talking quietly as if he didn't want the others to hear.

"Look Al- if you need some back-up and just don't want the chick to come, wink now and I'll follow you out of here." he whispered not at all quietly.

"Aaron, you know I can hear you! I will beat your ass!" Marcie yelled.

"Will you two stop, it's just me and Henry on this one- we've already decided that. I need you both here in case Sham-Bon makes a move."

Ardmon spoke up, "Moreno, if you'll follow me we have a vehicle ready for you at the gate."

Al nodded at the strong man who began to walk out towards the main gate. Alfred made as if to follow right away but Marcie stepped in front of him.

"Look just...just be safe, okay?" she hesitated for a moment and then quickly kissed the side of his cheek.

Al felt his cheeks grow a shade redder and he couldn't help but smile.

"Hey, more save the planet, less kissy-kissy. For real though Moreno, be careful out there." Flux joked then spoke seriously to his fellow Rift Resolver.

Alfred nodded firmly to him and he looked once more to Marcie before walking out to the main gate. He soon came to the doors and the guard on standby opened it for him to walk through. Ardmon stood in front of a small narrow vehicle with one wheel in the front and another in the back.

"She's not the flashiest, but she gets around good on the dirt roads out here. Trust me, this baby and I have been on some wild rides through these forests." Ardmon explained to Al. He seemed to have an emotional attachment to the motorbike.

Alfred climbed onto the leather seat and turned the ignition. The engine fired into action slowly and then idled with a repeated low rumble. Al gripped the handlebars and prepared to turn the throttle in his right hand. He tucked the energy revolver Papari had loaned him into the back of his pants and took off down the dirt path calling behind him to Ardmon.

"I'll try to bring her back in one piece!"

"What! YOU BETTER MORENO!" the large man boomed back, but Al was already halfway down the path and out of earshot.

He listened closely as Henry told him when to turn left and right down intersecting roads. They went on like this for hours until it seemed to Al that the path was growing narrower and the trees were growing thicker. Hemphion's sun was now high in the sky, marking just past mid-day.

"Take a right up ahead! " Henry called gleefully from his jacket pocket.

"Right? Where!" Al replied, frantically applying the brakes.

They certainly weren't the best brakes in the world, but Al managed to pull the motorbike to a stop before they wrecked into the dense trees before him. Alfred looked around him, it seemed as if they had reached a dead end.

"Henry what are you talking about, take a right? I don't see a path anywhere."

"Over there sir!" the A.I. flashed a golden beam of light onto the forest floor to Alfred's right.

Sure enough there was a very narrow path between the trees and brush. It was far too tight of a gap to get the motorbike through. Alfred turned the key and tossed it into his pants pocket.

"Looks like we're walking from here."

"You're walking, I just get to sit comfortably in my pocket!"

Alfred let out a small snort of laughter as he began to walk down the path. It curved from time to time when the trees became so dense that it was unavoidable, but for the most part it seemed to be leading them into the heart of the forest. The sun had gradually begun to lower in the sky and was now beginning to set. The small amount of light that was able to pass through the canopy of leaves was also steadily growing dimmer. Alfred pulled Henry out of his pocket and the A.I. illuminated the path ahead with a soft gold glow.

"Sir!" Henry shouted quite suddenly.

Alfred froze, "What Henry, what is it?"

"Up ahead there, in the bushes- look sir they're trembling!" Henry sounded frightened and turned off his light.

"Henry! What the hell, now it's dark! That made this ten times worse, turn the light back on!" Alfred lectured the scared A.I.

Al pointed Henry directly at the bushes that were now shaking furiously and Henry shined a bright light.

"Hey now, no need to make an old man more blind than he already is! Come on, enough with that light!" an old man had emerged from the shaking brush.

Henry lowered his brightness level and Al moved him down out of the man's face. In one hand he carried a lantern while the other hung free by his side. He had on strange robe, much different from the members of the village. It was so long that the end looked like it had been dragged across the ground for some time. The robe was made of a satin material and was purple with stars patterned all across it in intricate ways.

"Who are you?" Alfred asked, no longer feeling as threatened now that he saw it was an old man.

"Me? Who are *you*?" he asked.

"My name's Alfred Moreno, I'm a Rift Resolver. I'm looking for some people known as the Gazers?"

"HA! The Gazers, the Gazers, the Gaaaaaazers. The *all-knowing* Gazers- yes well they know it all, alright! They know we're all going to blow up!" the old man raised and lowered his voice and spoke as if he were half-crazed.

"Um...alright. We're going to go away now." Alfred said as he slowly backed away from the old man, who was now lifting his lantern up as if to get a better look at his face.

"Why would you leave now? You say you're in search of the *Gazers*, now don't you? Well there's one right here in front of you! HA HA!" the man shouted to Alfred, who temporarily paused his escape.

"So I guess Mother Via was right. You guys really are a waste of time. Alright, well I've gotta go back to the village and find a way to create a new sun." Alfred turned as if to head back down the path but the old man yelled to him.

"What's that you say? New sun?" the old man seemed confused.

"Yeah that's right." Al turned around. "The thing is, I need some help figuring out how to do it. I do have the Crystal of Gosia though." Al flashed a grin at the old man, pulling out the glimmering gold crystal and extending his arm out to show it to him.

The Gazer's eyes lit up in a newfound emotion when he saw the crystal.

"It can't be! You've really got it, the Crystal of Gosia!"

"That's right, now how's about you show me to the rest of the Gazers so we can figure out how to save this planet before it gets any darker."

"Ahhh yes, I will show you. But I must admit I'm no Gazer myself, simply their friendly messenger. I haven't had much messaging to do lately, but now I can bring you I suppose."

"Yeah, just uh, try to be a little less creepy if you could." Al shot him a strange look.

The messenger ignored his comment and instead stated, "The Gazers though, they won't be happy I've brought you here. They have been ordered to turn away everyone who comes here seeking knowledge for the past several months."

"Ordered? But by who? I was under the impression Gazers listened only to their god." Al questioned as he followed the slow old man deeper into the forest.

"That damned man! Sham-Bon *HUCK*!" he spat out the last name as if it disgusted him.

"What?!" Alfred stopped in bewilderment, "You mean Sham-Bon's the one who's forced the Gazers to abandon their people?"

"Yes, yes. That's right. That corrupt, rotten-filthy man. It wasn't too long ago, as I was saying. The previous head of the Huck Family passed away, and Sham-Bon being his only heir, took the throne. That's when things got bad. His father, Maztef, had always been good to the common men across Hemphion. But his son...Sham-Bon has forever been obsessed with converting Hemphion back to a monarchy and getting rid of the Parliament altogether. It is on this agenda that he has forced the Gazers to turn away any who come near them, otherwise he would have them killed. Many across our planet chose to die, but there are a few temples left where Gazers still abide. The one I'm taking you to now has only two members left, and I'm afraid you may not have much hope of convincing them of anything."

"I can't believe it. Sham-Bon's been doing all this just to become king of the planet!"

"Precisely. But it is funny how things work out isn't it? Because the only thing I see here is irony, pure irony in its finest form! Don't you *see*? Sham-Bon wasted his life trying to take over control of a planet that is set to be utterly destroyed in just a little over a day! Years ago when Parliament ordered evacuation, he announced the Huck Family would be staying on Hemphion! Broadcasts full of propaganda all over the television, all over the radio, everywhere! *Sham-Bon Huck Claims To Be Able To Save Hemphion From Exploding Sun!* And he won over almost everyone left on the planet! Just for not abandoning them and claiming to be able to save the world. If you weren't from Bratvia or an anarchist you probably bowed your head to the king."

They had begun walking again and Alfred was starting to feel a little overwhelmed, but he knew he had to focus on the new sun first and then he could deal with Sham-Bon and his plans afterward.

"And do you want to know what's even more ironic?" the man looked over at Alfred with his droopy bloodshot eyes.

"What's that?" Alfred asked, beginning to feel disturbed.

"If you do manage to save the planet and create a new sun, even if you do all of that- Sham-Bon will have gotten exactly what he wanted! The Parliament would never be able to return and earn the respect of the people. He would rule them all, and because of *you,* people would consider him their savior- thinking he had saved the planet himself!"

"That's where you've got it wrong old man. I'm going to get this planet a new sun and then I'll expose the Huck Family and Sham-Bon to the whole world."

the determination in Al's voice rang out through the forest.

"Well...we shall see what happens I suppose, soon enough too! Come now, we're almost there." the old man spoke to Alfred with a new tone of respect and continued to lead the way through the forest.

At last they broke through a patch of particularly sharp bramble and crawled out into a large clearing. In the center was a smallish structure. It was as if the center was the shape of a sphere and then it had several different little rooms sprouting off of it in random places. Alfred counted nine of the strange rooms sticking off as they walked through a raggedy garden toward the front door.

The messenger opened the heavy stone door through the use of a handle carved into the rock. They entered into a large open space with a towering-high ceiling that curved into a circular opening in the roof. One of Hemphion's moons could be seen in the sky above. Al could now see where the different rooms that stuck out on the outside were. Although they went all the way up near the top of the building, Alfred saw no way in which to get to the rooms on the upper levels.

"Wait here a moment while I try and get one of these old coots to come out here." the old man said as he led Alfred to the center of the circular stone floor.

"I've had about enough of old coots lately." he muttered as he watched the old man slowly walk across the building toward a wooden door on the far side. The crazy messenger was obviously quite worn out from the walk in the forest.

While he waited, Alfred took a minute to look at the ground he stood on. There were grooves carved into the floor in circles around the room. They were thicker and deeper around the outside and grew smaller as they moved in to the center, like the stump of a fallen tree. Alfred was standing in the smallest circle, which was still about four feet in diameter. This circle was different, there was a painting of some sort on its surface. Alfred bent down to get a better look and a glint of light caught his eye. It was a painting of two moons, presumably Lats and Lux. In the center of each moon there was a blue gemstone embedded into the rock. The smaller moon, Lux, was beginning to reflect its light on the gem in its painting. Alfred tried to study it some more but a loud banging interrupted his thoughts and he stood and turned to see the old man had finally reached the door.

"Barnin! Barnin, come on out! Your faithful messenger has brought you some company! Barnin come out here already!" the man continued to knock his wrinkled fist repeatedly against the wooden door.

"Gummly you old fool I told you to leave here and not come back! You know we are to turn away all that come!" an angry voice sounded from within the room.

"But your Wiseness! It is a Rift Resolver that has come. He has the Blade and all! He demands to speak with the Gazers!"

"I don't give a damn if it's the emperor of the galaxy! Send him away and you begone as well!" the voice called back rudely.

The old man turned and shrugged at Alfred as if he didn't know what more he could do.

"You said there were two of them here didn't you? Well, where's the other?" Alfred asked in frustration.

"Ah yes...Wardriff. He tends to wander in the night."

"This is a mess, I've wasted so much time." Alfred said to himself.

"Shall we go now sir?" Henry asked as if he really wanted his friend to say yes.

Alfred thought for a moment. This was the best lead he had, if he returned now he wouldn't have a clue how to create a new sun and there'd be no time to figure it out. Lats was beginning to come into view beside Lux in the circle above him.

"No. I'll force it out of this bastard if I have to." he finally replied, rage flaring up in his eyes.

Henry flashed his lights in distress a few times as Alfred stalked up to the door.

Reaching it, he turned to Gummly saying sharply, "Get out of the way old man."

The man grumbled a bit and shifted over from in front of the door. Alfred banged his fist hard against the wood, causing the sound to echo around the temple.

"Listen up Barnin! My name's Al Moreno, Rift Resolver. I need to ask you something urgent, it could mean the salvation of your planet!"

"Ha! Salvation, what a joke." came the answer from behind the door. "Don't come bothering me on my last night alive on this world with such senseless blibber-blabber!"

Alfred paused his pounding on the door for a moment and took a deep breath. He stood back a few steps and then charged at the door- ramming it hard with his right shoulder. The wood cracked and splintered a bit but still held firm in its frame. Al quickly picked himself up off the floor.

"Quit that! Can't you let an old man die in peace?" the voice wailed from inside.

Alfred reached behind him and gripped the energy revolver in his hand. He raised it so it pointed at the center of the door.

"What are you doing with *that?*" Gummly gulped nervously beside him.

"I hope you're not standing behind that door you bastard!" he yelled and not two moments later squeezed the trigger- blasting an energy round into the door.

The wood splintered and broke into pieces, making it so that only a few wooden planks remained hanging in the upper section of the frame. From inside something sounded as if it had thudded onto the floor, causing several items to clang and bounce onto the stone ground. An abrupt holler sounded shortly after.

"You coming out here Barnin, buddy? Or you want me to come in there and drag you out?" Al shouted.

"Yes, enough- put that thing away for Saturn's sake!" the man whined as he crawled underneath the remaining fragments of the door. He stood up and began to pat the dust and dirt off of the robe he was wearing, which was very similar to the one Gummly had on.

Alfred lowered his revolver and tucked it back into his pants, studying the man as he did so. He was quite tall, an inch or two above Alfred even and had a surprisingly reddish beard for a man of his age. His face drooped and wrinkled around his nose and cheeks, but he appeared to be in good health. On his head sat a purple bucket hat from which fine wisps of gray hair dangled out of. He took a moment to straighten it on his head before looking at Alfred.

"Well you've got me out here boy! Tell me what it is you want so badly so I can get back to spending the rest of my last night in peace!"

"That's just it, this doesn't have to be your last night. I've brought the Crystal of Gosia, I just need to figure out how I can use it to create a new sun for Hemphion. What do you know of these things, can you be of any help?" Alfred interrogated the man quickly.

Barnin's eyes seemed to spark with interest for a moment at the mention of the crystal, but this quickly passed and his face furrowed back into a scowl.

"What of the crystal you fool? To create a new sun, it is only the work for a god! And little use *they* are, we've come to learn. Completely abandoned." he shook his head and his words carried with them a spiteful resonance.

Alfred was growing steadily more annoyed as the man spoke, but he decided to take a different approach.

"Who is this god of yours? Everyone here says he has abandoned the people of this planet- well what is he called; you Gazers receive omens from him do you not?"

"Omens! Haven't glimpsed one in years, not once since those good-for-nothing men of Sham-Bon came in here telling us to turn away all those who seek our god's wisdom! Well our god is a fool and I reject him- reject him entirely! He deserves no name!" the man ranted with a passionate wrath Alfred hadn't seen before.

The men turned at the sound of yet another ancient-looking man's voice. He was hunched over a short wooden cane and was dressed in the same clothes as Barnin, only he wore no hat and left his bald head exposed.

"Barnin! To speak of our Almighty, our Infinite Spirit- in such a manner! Do you wish to go to the underworld in a day's time? Our god is Hashish, the all-knowing!" the man pushed his dry raspy voice to the point where it cracked several times while scowling at his associate.

"What do you know of it, you lunatic? Your mind has gone to mush!" Barnin insulted back quickly.

"It is true I may not be as sharp as I once was, but my faith in our Lord will never waver! Come now boy, you say you have the Crystal of Gosia- well let me see it!"

Alfred reached into his pocket and removed the crystal, holding it up for the Gazer to see and asking, "I take it you're Wardriff then?"

"Glimmering Galaxies Barnin! The boy has brought with him the crystal, you know what this means!" Wardriff shuffled over to stand nearer to the others.

"It means nothing you imbecile. We have no god, he turned his back on us when we needed his guidance the most." Barnin lectured.

Alfred's mind sparked with the tiniest inkling of hope as he asked, "What does it mean? I can save Hemphion, can't I?"

"You? Hardly I'd say...to create an entirely new sun and remove the one set to explode is a feat only for gods. But the crystal- you are aware it works as a gateway into the godly realms?"

By now both Lux and Lats were radiating a brilliant silver glow onto the stone floor.

"I only knew that it could work as a passageway to Gosia. So this Hashish, you say he's turned his back on Hemphion? Well if it's true that I can speak to him, you must tell me how- it might be the only chance we have."

"I will have no part in this, you are all ignorant naive fools who cling to false hope." snorted Barnin who began to walk back into his room.

"Nevermind him. That Blade- it must mean you are indeed a Rift Resolver, a man who serves to correct the wrongdoings of others in protection of the Universe. Come now, you must hurry to the center while Lax and Luts lights continue to illuminate their gemstones."

Alfred, having no other choice, decided to trust the strange Gazer. He ran quickly to the center of the floor and Wardriff and Gummly followed and stood nearby.

Alfred crouched on the painting in the innermost circle. The gemstones in each image of the moons were now reflecting brightly with the same silver color of Lux and Lat's beams.

"What now?" he looked frantically to Wardriff who stood hunched over his cane.

"You know better than I do! Open the gateway- set that crystal between the gemstones and do whatever it is you must do! Come now boy, hurry before the light passes out of the skylight!"

Alfred fumbled with the crystal in his hands, setting it on floor between the shimmering stones. He quickly pulled his Rift Blade from his belt and crouched on both knees, raising it high above his head before slamming the tip into Gosia's golden crystal. Just as the blade tapped the surface of the crystal; the moons' light seemed to flash with a brightness that filled up the entire temple and forced Alfred to close his eyes for fear he'd go blind. He felt the same odd sensation as before. It was as if his soul had leaped against his body- thrusting him into the bright light he was trying desperately to shield his eyes from. He felt himself being pulled into it and just before everything went black he heard Gummly's voice calling out loudly.

"Good luck lad!"

10 THE FATHER OF TWO MOONS

This time was different. There was no wonderfully painted tunnel of colors. Alfred saw nothing but black, but he could feel that he was being sucked violently through the void. His body lurched and swung as if he were limp, and the terrible sensation of his soul lurching against his body was now becoming almost unbearable.

Suddenly a circle of light appeared, no Alfred realized, there were two of them. The horrifying sensation of his body fighting to keep in his soul had stopped and he now found himself to be standing. He looked down at his feet which seemed be standing on the darkness that encircled everything but the light of the two circles. Frantically, he patted his inner jacket pocket and let out a sigh of relief when he felt Henry. He pulled him out and held him in his palm.

"Henry- are you alright?" he asked the A.I.

There was no response, and no indications of lights or anything else flashing on the golden egg.

"Henry, you there? C'mon buddy I'm going to need your help." Al was beginning to panic, something wasn't right.

"His kind cannot gain entry to this realm." one circle of light spoke.

"Who is that, who's talking? What've you done with Henry?" Alfred demanded- shouting at the circles of light. He noticed that one was slightly smaller than the other.

"You...you're Lux and Lats. Hemphion's moons."

"Ah an intelligent human, how nice." Lats replied in a higher pitched voice than his brother.

"You've got to let me see Hashish." Alfred insisted.

"You hear that brother? A human actually *wants* to see father! And to think we thought no one liked him anymore."

"Yes well I assume he has his reasons Lats. Very well Alfred Moreno, but don't blame us when you feel the wrath of our father's temper. He can be quite...how would you describe him brother?"

"Oh father? Yes well he can get a bit *heated* sometimes one might say." Lats snickered as he finished speaking.

Lux laughed at his brother's comment and then commanded the man before them.

"One step forward Rift Resolver. Only one. Any farther and you will burn up before you utter a single word!"

"Burn up?" Alfred asked, but he was once again surrounded in complete darkness. The moons had disappeared.

"One step it is I guess." and he took it.

An incredible flare of heat scorched through Alfred's body. He screamed in agony and reached his hands to his face, which felt as if it were beginning to melt off his skull. Then just as suddenly as it had come, it was gone. Now rid of the horrendous pain he looked around him. In front of him was an enormous red ball comprised of bubbling magma and fire. Everything else was black. Wait no, Alfred thought, there are the slightest glimmers of stars hidden amongst the darkness.

"Where am I?" he said aloud.

Something was moving on the blazing ball of light, it appeared that there was a giant stream of fire that was rushing directly at Alfred. He made as if to run away but then remembered that Lux had said to take only one step. So he did all he could to force his body from running away as the flames rushed at him in a tornado of fire. Alfred closed his eyes tight, clenching every muscle in his body. He expected death. But the moment had passed when the flames should have annihilated him, so slowly he opened his eyes.

It had become hotter than it was a moment before. At first there was too much blinding light to make out anything at all. Then Al's eyes adjusted and he saw a man in front of him with a body comprised of fire. What's more, the man had no legs but rather just a head and torso of flames that combined into the tornado of fire leading back to the burning ball of light. Alfred was able to see his eyes for just a moment. There was no mistaking the hostility within them.

Then pain. Excruciating, tormenting pain that Alfred thought was surely about to kill him. But yet again it stopped and he remained standing.

"Please." Alfred began, but was yet again radiated with the skin-melting misery.

Alfred, surviving still, coughed madly- feeling as if his throat had been doused in gasoline with a match thrown in as a chaser.

"What is this? Why have you not died? I demand to know- who is he that thinks himself worthy enough to be in the presence of Hashish The Sun?"

"Sun…? You mean you're the sun?" Alfred was beginning to understand- the ball of burning light in front of him must be Hemphion's Sun. And this man, this fire-man, must be Hashish. The god who the Gazers claimed to have abandoned them. They were one.

"What a foolish question to ask! I am Hashish The Sun, I have just told you this. Tell me, what are you and why does your soul not utterly incinerate when I blast you with unbearable heat?" Hashish replied, glaring suspiciously at Alfred.

Alfred coughed in an attempt to sooth his burning throat, and then answered.

"My name is Al Moreno. I'm a Rift Resolver. Why my soul isn't incinerating- that I'm not really sure of. I don't even understand how my body's not complete ash by now, but I'm definitely okay with it."

"You have no body. Bodies are not able to pass through the gate and so they are left behind while the soul comes alone. As for why your soul does not perish from my power- this I do not know. Why is it you have come here?" Hashish explained, crossing his arms and narrowing his eyes at Alfred.

That must be why Henry couldn't come through- he must not have a soul, Alfred thought.

"So then Hashish, seeing as you are the sun, won't you be blowing up here soon? Like tomorrow soon?"

"This! This wretched ignorance, this blatant disrespect, I cannot tolerate this! It infuriates me, and they wonder why I turn my back! They turned theirs first!" the fire that made up the god's body grew taller and burned hotter as he spoke in rage.

"What do you mean this ignorance?" Alfred asked, puzzled.

"This lie, this blasphemy! To think that I, Hashish The Sun, would explode? Never I say- not until the Universe forces me. And even then I'll put up a fight."

"But if you're not going to explode that means Hemphion is saved! Wait, no this- this was all plotted by-"

"Sham-Bon." Hashish said the word as if it were the most wicked name he had ever uttered.

"But why do you say that your people have abandoned you? I was just with a Gazer, a man who still believed and defended you!"

"A Gazer? There are no Gazers left, only cowardice fools who slandered my name by turning away those who sought my guidance and wisdom. Listening to a creature like that, a horrid soul, like Sham-Bon. Failing to protect the ways I set down for them so long ago. And now they bend at his will, do anything he says- as if *he* is their god. The people have lost their faith in me as a result of the Gazers' ignorance."

"But not all of them have lost their faith, I've been to an entire village where the people praise you still. They continue to stand against the Huck Family and Sham-Bon."

Hashish's face twisted up for a moment and Alfred thought he was about to get scorched again. But then the flames of his face came back in a smile followed by cackling laughter.

"One village, you say? Half of the planet will have by now put their faith in that of one individual- that despicable man. Can't you see I can do nothing to stop it either? My light has by now begun to shine all across the Western Hemisphere and they will all be celebrating in Sham-Bon, believing that he has saved the planet from my destruction. And yet, what could I do? If I never shined my light again, they would all perish. I must admit I toyed with the idea of it for awhile, but I came to decide that I'd rather have the people be alive than prove one man to be a fake."

"Then you do care, you have not abandoned your people- you did all that you could to protect them, even at the cost of them losing their faith in you."

For the first time the fiery god seemed not to know what to say. The look of despise had been replaced with a wistful gaze. The god grunted and then dipped his head at Alfred. The Rift Resolver was taken aback at the sign of respect from the god, and even more so when Hashish began to speak again.

"The Universe decided well in allowing you to join the ranks of the Rift Society. Then again, as much as I hate to say it, the Universe is never truly wrong- we all just act a part in its long-premeditated script. Now, Al Moreno, it is time for you to go back. Occurences in your realm are in need of your participation."

Hashish looked as if he were about to send Al back to the waking world, but the Rift Resolver spoke up quickly.

"Wait! If I manage to stop Sham-Bon it would restore the people's faith in you! You have only to do one thing, reopen communications with the Gazers and tell them that you are Hashish The Sun, and that you will not be exploding and have not turned your back on your people. I'll take care of the Huck Family."

Hashish rolled his eyes and Alfred noticed for the first time that his appearance was modeled after a younger looking man.

"Ugh, those guys? They're so boring at times, but I suppose you're right. That might do the trick. Alright, now you better return before it's too late. As I said, there are events tugging for your presence back on Hemphion. One step backwards, try hard not to do the opposite!" he laughed and looked as if he were about to absorb back into the sun but turned around one more time.

"Oh and it'll be hard to kill Sham-Bon, but that is the only way to assure this all works. Take my word as a god, he is a man who has done things that deserve punishments far worse than death. Then again, you're not human either so I suppose it may be a fair fight! May the best win, good-luck Moreno- I'm rooting for you!" and with that Hashish opened his mouth and blew a great flame that forced Alfred to stumble back.

The moment his foot landed on the dark ground behind him he felt himself drop and fall down through the darkness. He thought he could hear the laughter of Hashish in the direction of the sun as he fell away from it. He felt as if he were falling faster than a spacecraft in hyper-speed. Suddenly he saw two great discs of light, realizing that it must be Lux and Lats. They seemed to glow at him with a new curiosity, but said nothing as he fell further down past them. Alfred was now beginning to make out the fast-approaching surface of Hemphion. Faster and faster his soul flew towards the face of the planet.

Alfred paid no attention to the fact that he would soon be rushing back into his body at insane speeds, his mind was focused on one thing. Hashish had said

"You're not human either" and had been unable to burn up his soul after many attempts. It had hurt like a bitch, he thought, but it hadn't killed him.

"What am I?" he said and then quickly turned his words into a scream as he realized he was flying through the skylight in the Gazer's temple back into his body. His body that was currently struggling to be lifted off of the stone floor by three old men and a little golden egg.

11 RACE TO THE VILLAGE

Alfred felt his soul crash into his body, forcing him to open his eyes and begin taking in refreshing gulps of air.

"Sir, you're alive!" Henry cheered from where he sat on the ground beside him.

Alfred looked up at the three shocked old men and proclaimed, "Well, put me down already will ya?" they subsequently dropped him roughly onto the floor.

"It's impossible!" announced Barnin, who had come back into the center of the temple when he saw the bright flash of light.

"You've seen Hashish then, what has he to say- are we saved?" Wardriff questioned.

"You need know nothing more than this." Alfred sat up off the ground and tucked Henry and the Crystal of Gosia back into his jacket pocket. "Your god has not abandoned you, or at least he hasn't anymore- and the sun was never going to explode! It's all been a part of Sham-Bon's plan to bring power back to the Huck Family. How he managed to pull of such a rumor that the sun was going to explode, that I don't know. But by doing so he cleared out

Parliament, and by 'saving' Hemphion he'll gain the trust of all its people."

Barnin looked to be profoundly flabbergasted at the very idea that their god had in fact not abandoned them, but that this was all a giant lie formulated by a greedy man. Gummly reached out and poked a wrinkled finger into Alfred's side, as if he weren't convinced the man was actually alive. Alfred flinched away at his touch and shot him an annoyed look.

"You had no pulse. No sign of breathing. No oxygen to the brain for damn near twenty minutes! And you're perfectly fine…" he seemed beyond confused.

"Yes, well it's a good thing I am. Look I've got to go now and return to Bratvia, I fear Sham-Bon is going to have it destroyed since it's the last village who stands against him."

Bang!

The noise of an energy gun sounded from outside the temple's main doors.

"Gazers, open this door! By order of the Royal Huck Military you must be taken into protective custody immediately."

"Quick, you three get out of here. Run and don't let them find you. Then, if I can pull this off, you must once again accept the omens and spread the word of Hashish amongst your people."

Wardriff's lips softened into a warm smile and he looked at Alfred gratefully. The hunched over man was oddly the most well put together during those quick minutes before two of Sham-Bon's men swung open the heavy stone door. He quickly ushered a speechless Barnin and a muttering Gummly over to the side of the temple wall. Alfred watched in amazement as the old man tapped his cane twice on the ground, and the rock under where they stood rose up until it came to a stop outside one of the higher-up rooms in the temple. Alfred had no time to ask how Wardriff had done it, and as the doors began to open he directed Henry to remain on the ground. Then, pulling his energy revolver out, he dove just to the left side of the door and stood flat against the wall. The ground that Wardriff had forced to rise up had now sunken back to perfect level within the floor.

"Hey! Where is everybody, what's going on?" one of the men yelled into the room, his voice echoing around the empty space.

"Look, there in the center! Is that gold?" the other man began to run towards Henry in excitement.

"Wait no! It might be a--" the first man never finished what he was about to say.

Instead, two things happened almost simultaneously. The guard who ran eagerly towards Henry tried to stop himself, but before he could the golden egg blasted small beam of light that went into his forehead, all the way through his brain, and out the backside. He dropped to the floor- dead.

At the same time, Alfred had run up behind the man's companion and put the gun to his head. While pulling the trigger he finished the first guard's warning, "A trap?"

"Go on then boy- waste no more time!" Wardriff called from the room high up near the temple ceiling.

Alfred looked up and nodded, then grabbed Henry and ran out the temple doors.

"They must have had a vehicle- yes there! Henry can you start it?" Alfred asked hurriedly as he saw the covered four-wheel vehicle in front of him. It was still quite small and looked as if it only sat two people side by side, but appeared to have tires that could crawl over rough terrain.

"Absolutely sir." Henry assured him and as Alfred climbed into the driver's seat the engine rumbled to life with a loud roar and a poof of exhaust smoke.

Alfred could see where the Huck men had come up from a different trail than the one Gummly had taken him through. This path was just wide enough for the vehicle to fit down, and Alfred took it not knowing where it led to.

"I'm going to need some navigation here buddy. By the way, I learned two other things while I was visiting with Hashish. You want the good or the bad news first?" he called to his A.I. friend.

In between giving a frenzy of directions, Henry managed to reply saying, "Let's have the bad."

"You have no soul."

"Oh...oh my. I'm afraid I don't quite know what to say. What's the good news?" Henry asked, flashing a light on the right side of Alfred's face to indicate an upcoming turn.

"The good news is, you're not the only one who found out some crazy stuff. Rumor is I'm not exactly human. Or if I am, my soul must be flame-resistant!"

"Well sir, what do you think of it all?" Henry asked nervously.

"I think we focus on getting back to the village as soon as possible. Hashish hinted that something awful might be happening and I'm beginning to get that vibe myself.

"Yes sir, shall I optimize the vehicle's software for speed?" Henry announced, delighted to have such an optimistic friend.

"That's what I'm talking about!" Al hollered as the vehicle seemed to thrust forward with even more power than before.

Soon enough the vehicle was cruising at high speed around an enormously-curved dirt road that cut between the trees. They continued to follow it for some time before Alfred abruptly slammed the brakes, forcing the vehicle to skid to a stop in the middle of the road.

"Over there Henry, I think that's where I left the motorbike."

"Forget the motorbike sir! It's probably been found by Huck men by now anyway!" the A.I. responded indignantly.

Ignoring his sidekick, Alfred proceeded to climb out of the vehicle and began walking through the trees. Alfred was right about the motorbike, but Henry had also been correct in guessing there would be some of Sham-Bon's men standing guard in front of it. They were likely waiting to see if anyone came back to retrieve it.

"Let me handle this Henry- I can't leave Ardmon's bike behind."

Alfred cleared his throat as he stepped out into view of the guards.

"Hey there boys- great job watching over the bike, I'll be needing to head out immediately- you know how much patience the boss has!" he spoke to the guards in a friendly tone as if he had known them for years and they had been doing him a great favor by watching the bike.

They each raised their gun and pointed it at Al as one of them called out, "And who are you?"

"Fellas, fellas! Easy with who you're aiming those guns at now. The name's Al- Aaron Flux." he corrected quickly with a cough, "Rift Resolver, working with Sham-Bon to save the planet from the exploding sun, you know?"

The guards lowered their guns slightly and the other now spoke up.

"I didn't know anything about a Rift Resolver working with Sham-Bon, what about you?" he turned to the other guard who shook his head in response.

"Well of course you don't know! No offense you two, I'm sure you're both men of great service to the Huck Family, but Sham-Bon can't just go around telling everyone something as secret as this mission! Now come on, you've already made me late- I don't want to have to write you two up- you seem like nice guys." Alfred explained.

"That does makes sense." one of them said, seemingly taken-aback at the thought of getting written up by someone working closely with Sham-Bon.

"We're sorry to have held you up Mr. Flux." the other apologized quickly and they moved aside for Alfred to get on the bike.

Just as Alfred climbed onto the seat and turned the key in the ignition, one of the men's radios began to chatter.

"Section 7 be aware that we have just found two dead men in the Gazer's temple. Be on the lookout for a young male, brown hair, wearing a leather jacket. We have reason to believe he may be armed and a trained member of the Rift Society. Over."

"Well that's my cue to go!" Alfred shouted at the men beside him, who attempted to dive and grab the handle bars from his control.

Henry flashed a quick beam of light into the nearest one's face, and Alfred turned the throttle hard-sending the bike flying down the dirt road he had originally come from. All was clear, but not for long. Al soon heard the rumbling of an engine behind them and Henry warned that the Huck men were in pursuit.

"Damn, why can't these people ever just relax. Like hey, maybe today I won't follow the orders of the most evil man on the planet. But nooo, they have to come chasing after me and now I'm left with no other choice but to make sure they don't catch up." Alfred complained, still tearing down the path ahead.

"My sympathies sir." Henry flashed.

Glancing in one of the small mirrors that extended off either side of the bike, Al could see the guards were approaching quickly in a similar vehicle to the one they had hijacked before. The one that had tried to knock him off of the bike was driving and the other had climbed up top, behind what Alfred quickly discovered was a mounted gun. He tried to zig-zag his steering as he heard the turret begin to spray out bullets. One of the rounds burst into his right shoulder. It wasn't energy ammo, he thought, but damn it still didn't feel good. Suddenly the handle-bars began to fight against his control and it seemed as if the motor-bike was now driving itself.

"I'll cover driving and keep the bullets off of you sir! You take care of our tail!" Henry announced, apparently responsible for the bike's auto-steering.

Alfred was now left to focus on only two things-maintaining his balance on the ever-swerving vehicle, and aiming his energy revolver at the men chasing after them. The Rift Resolver did a full turn, swinging his legs around so that he faced the fast-approaching men. The look on the man's face who had shot him was full of surprise as he noticed that the bike was evidently driving itself. Alfred took full advantage, and closing one eye took aim on the enemy's front left tire. He joined his other hand to form a steadier shot and then fired a round that landed just in front of the vehicle- creating a massive hole in the road. The all-terrain car took a sharp dip into the hole, but continued to crawl after them.

"Sir, I can't avoid that bullet range for much longer- my calculations show that the probability of you getting hit increases every twenty seconds that we are continued to be chased."

"Well, I guess if I'm not quite human I might as well make use of it. Henry, when I say to- hit the brakes on the bike, but don't throw me off!"

"Sir! Are you sure?" the A.I. asked fearfully.

"Yes, ready? One...two..." Alfred began counting.

"Wait sir, I am unfamiliar with this counting- when do I apply the brakes?"

"Three Henry! It's always on THREE!" Alfred almost went flying over the front of the bike as Henry decided to slam the brakes.

Alfred had no time to be angry at his friend's timing, he leaned his body weight forward as quickly as he could, just barely managing to stay on the motorbike. They had come to a complete stop in the road. Alfred winced as he felt an array of bullets fly into his lower stomach, but kept his eyes focused on the front hood of the vehicle that was now about to hit him head-on.

"He stopped! The brakes, the BRAKES!" the guard on top yelled frantically down to the driver.

It looked as if Alfred and the motorbike were about to get smashed to bits. He didn't know how much stress his body would allow, but he was guessing getting hit by a car at high-speed wasn't going to end well for him. Alfred reached his arm back, and sent his Rift Blade flying through the air. He froze and watched, knowing if he missed he was about to endure an insane amount of pain. The Blade swung in circles through the air, and finally came to rest when it stuck deep into the metal hood of the enemy's ride. A bright flash of light emitted, and Alfred allowed a shout of triumph to escape as the entire vehicle and the men in it disappeared into a Rift portal.

"Always been better with a knife than a gun." he admitted, walking a few steps into the road behind him and picking his Rift Blade up off the ground.

"We need to work on our timing Alfred!" Henry exclaimed.

"*You* need to work on *your* timing Henry." Al laughed as he got back onto the bike and continued to drive toward the village of Bratvia.

The rest of journey back went by without much action. As the first rays of the sun could be seen climbing over the horizon, they were nearing their destination. Henry broke the long silence after a while.

"Sir, where do all those things go that you throw your Rift Blade into?" he asked curiously.

"Well it depends- I decide that when I use the Blade. In this case, I don't think anyone's going to be seeing those two for a long time. They're on the planet Dirdock, light years away."

Henry let out a robotic laugh before asking, "Isn't that in the Galactic Waste Sector?"

"That's right. Those two are on garbage duty. Or they're under a mountain of garbage suffocating as we speak, I can't really choose the location that precisely."

Henry laughed harder in his bot-like cheerful voice, and Alfred couldn't help but chuckle with him for a moment. They rode on for a bit longer before Henry lit up in his pocket again, but there was no more laughter in the A.I.'s voice when he spoke.

"Alfred, the emergency alarm has just been activated in Bratvia."

Alfred's face hardened into a serious look as he replied, "Come on, we have to get back as fast as possible. Sham-Bon's begun his assault."

12 A BATTLE FOR BRATVIA

Hemphion's sun had now risen above the tall treetops of the forest that concealed Bratvia within its midst. Alfred was met promptly by Ardmon outside the main gate of the village wall, which he opened for him to drive through. Another villager quickly shut the gates behind them. An alarm pierced through the air throughout the inside of the compound.

"My friends, quickly- can you take me to them?"

"Yes but we've received a warning from our scouts on the northern road that an army of Huck men are now approaching Bratvia's walls."

"I know, it's Sham-Bon- he's trying to silence this last village. Take me to the others, I'll explain then." Alfred gave Ardmon a looked filled with urgency.

The hulking man nodded and led him hastily to Mother Via's sanctuary. As Alfred stepped into the courtyard he was immediately met with a firm embrace from Marcie. After a moment she released him. Alfred could see the mixed emotions in her eyes.

"You've done it! You've got us a new sun!" her excitement faded into concern as she noticed the blood that was covering his clothes. "Alfred, what's the matter- have you been shot? Where did all this blood come from?"

Alfred glanced down at his clothes for the first time since escaping from the two guards. The upper part of his pants and lower part of his undershirt were soaked in the thick red liquid. He lifted his shirt and jacket up swiftly, revealing no sign of the entry wounds he had received from the mounted gun's bullets.

"Look see, I'm fine. Don't worry about me now- we've got to get this place ready to stand against a full-on attack. Sham-Bon is going to try to wipe this place off of the face of the planet. He likely knows what I've found out and needs to get rid of all the evidence of his sinister plans."

"What plans? Glad to see you made it back alive Moreno." Flux asked, entering the courtyard followed by Mother Via.

Alfred gave them a short version of what had happened since he had seen them last. How he had visited with the people's god, Hashish, and that he no longer deserted them. That Hemphion's sun was actually perfectly fine, and it had all been falsated in order to force Parliament to evacuate the planet along with all those who stood by the government.

"Unbelievable." Flux stated when he had finished. "One man managed to convince an entire planet that their sun was going to explode?"

"That's right, I don't know how exactly. Other than the Huck Family is certainly not short of any resources. What's worse- now that the sun has risen everyone will believe he's the savior of the planet."

"That bastard. I've...I've wasted most of my life trying to find a way to save this planet. And all this time I should've just been trying to kill him." Marcie's eyes glowed with anger and despair.

"There's no time for regrets now." Alfred shot her a sympathetic look before turning back to the others. "Ardmon, can you help Mother Via get all the people who can't fight into the sanctuary? I'll need everyone else who can shoot an energy blaster to defend this place until I can get to Sham-Bon."

Ardmon nodded at the Rift Resolver's orders and headed out into the village, guiding Mother Via beside him.

"You really think Sham-Bon's going to come here himself?" Flux doubted.

"If he doesn't, I'll hunt him down. But we know he still wants the crystal for something, so my bet is he makes an appearance. Flux can you round up all the villagers who can fight?"

"You got it." came the reply as Aaron headed out after Ardmon into the village.

Alfred turned to look at Marcie who was staring at her feet. Walking closer to her, he gripped her armored shoulder softly with his right hand. She looked up at him with a gaze of defeat that remained stagnant in her eyes.

"Listen, I know you're shaken up. But I also know how much these people mean to you. This doesn't have to be the end damn it- I won't let it!" Alfred carried a face replete with defiance.

Marcie looked back at him, overwhelmed by his passion to save a planet he was only just visiting for the first time. Something tugged at Alfred's jacket sleeve and he turned to see Jashi, armed with a bow and arrow.

"I'm ready to fight!" he announced.

Alfred looked unsure of what to say, but Marcie crouched down and spoke to the boy.

"Good! Now I've got a very important job for you Jashi. You see those doors over there?" she pointed at the doors that led into the sanctuary.

Alfred looked up to see Ardmon and Mother Via leading a last group of helpless villagers into the crowded courtyard.

"Mhm!" Jashi acknowledged.

"You don't let anyone get through those doors okay? You've got to help Ardmon and the others who can fight protect this place and our people." she said fiercely to the child.

"I won't let you down." came the quick response, and Jashi ran over to meet up with Ardmon and a few other men who were armed with various weapons.

"So are you going to help me kill this bastard or what? He won't go down easy, Hashish informed me he's not exactly human." Al looked to Marcie who had now stood back up.

"Right, let's go." there was no sign of the dejection that had been in her eyes before.

The two of them hurried out of the sanctuary doors, which Ardmon sealed firmly behind them. Out front stood Aaron Flux with a few dozen rows of men standing beside him. Alfred noticed only a few of them carried energy guns, and most were armed with primitive weapons such as bows and spears. Marcie came to stand beside Flux as Alfred addressed the villagers.

"Alright, here's what we know: an army of Huck men are approaching from the North with the sole intention of eliminating every trace of this village. Those of you who don't have energy weapons will need to stay behind and prevent anyone from getting through the sanctuary's doors. The rest of you will follow Aaron and try to get a good position on top of the North-side wall. And if you see Sham-Bon don't waste your rounds- they won't be able to kill him. Leave that to us. Today is not the day Bratvia will fall, and neither will the planet of Hemphion to that son of a bitch's rule."

As Al finished speaking the men of Bratvia cheered and raised their weapons in the air. While the rest of the planet may have fallen into despair, they would stand against the evil of the Huck Family to the very end. After a few moments the men fell silent again and looked to Flux who Al had put in charge of them.

"Flux before you go," Alfred spoke once more to his friend. "Find out which one these men can travel the quickest through the forest and have him try to get word to the closest village. It may be hard to convince them, but we're going to need all the back-up we can get."

"Right, give Sham-Bon a punch or two for me will ya?" he called behind him with a grin as he began to lead the villagers toward the North wall.

Alfred and Marcie ran ahead of them down the main path leading through the buildings of the small compound. It didn't take long before they had reached the plasti-crete barrier. Alfred followed her quickly up one of the rope ladders that hung against its side. Reaching the top, Alfred saw something he had never faced before as a member of the Rift Society.

A few hundred yards out marched an enormous group of men. They were infantry soldiers of the royal army. Every single one of them looked to be armed to the fullest extent with energy weapons of all different varieties. Next came a massive tank, and behind this was just a slightly lesser unit of men from the first. High in the sky above them a magnificent warship was hovering slowly. Its metal surface gleamed with the reflected light of the sun, and energy cannons could be seen extending off the front.

"What now?" Marcie showed no sign of intimidation from the oncoming army of men and machines of destruction.

"Right. My bet's that warship up there- he'll likely be organizing the attack from somewhere on board."

"Okay...but how are we going to get all the way up there? Bratvia has nothing that can lift into the air and you've never been on the Iron Pinnacle before so you can't open a rift to it."

"Wait, the Iron Pinnacle? You mean you know this ship? Please tell me you've been on it before?!" Alfred asked excitedly.

"Well yeah that's where I did a lot of my training actually, but I don't see-"

"Climb onto my back." Marcie shot him a look like he was out of his mind. "Come on just trust me. If I open a rift and we enter the portal at the same time while in contact, we should be able to get on board since you've been there before. Now hurry, Henry let me ride on his back, there's no shame!"

Marcie smiled, amazed that Al was still able to crack a joke in this hour of dire emergency. She jumped onto his back as he pulled his blade from his belt and sliced through the air in front of them. Aaron and his men were now climbing up the wall around them, and a few of them looked in awe at the strange portal that had opened in front of the Rift Resolver.

"Ready?"

"Ready!" sung out Henry loudly before Marcie could answer.

Alfred centered their combined weight and leapt forward into the rift. They emerged only a fraction of a second later in a spacious white room. Marcie climbed off of Alfred's back.

"Well looks like I used my divine energy right, wasn't sure about that one. Never tried to rift onto a moving airship- let alone on one I've never set foot on before!" Alfred exclaimed.

"You're really something else. Come on, we need to figure out where Sham-Bon is." she replied.

The two of them ran out of the room through a door which slid up as they approached it. They had come out into a hallway that was constructed from the same white panels as the room they had been in. There was a large logo of the royal family's crest on one side of the wall. Below it read:

The Iron Pinnacle.

"Lead the way." Alfred instructed, following her closely down the length of the hall.

They took a right turn at an intersecting hallway and ran past several of the automated doors.

"Here!" Marcie shouted, pulling Alfred over to one of them. There was something strangely familiar about the blue light that glowed above it. Marcie pushed a button beside it several times but the door didn't open.

"Is this an elevator?" Alfred asked impatiently.

"Yeah but the button isn't working. Come on, there should be a flight of stairs somewhere around here."

"Wait no. These things are voice activated now- a little too voice activated if you ask me."

Marcie shot him a strange look but said nothing as Al looked up at the blue light and spoke to the elevator.

"Hey, hello there- Elevator? We'd like some service if you wouldn't mind."

The blue light flashed brightly and a familiar robotic voice spoke.

"Hello there sir! Ma'am! How can I be of service to you today?" the elevator asked gleefully.

"Elevator 041, is that you?" Alfred knew he had recognized the voice.

"I'm afraid you've mistaken me for a relative, sir. I'm Elevator 1167902345765! Elevator 041 is my fourteenth cousin, twice removed!" the A.I. rambled off its name and explained its relation to the other elevator in delight.

"Oh, sorry for the mix up. Anyway, do you think it'd be too much trouble to take us up to the command floor? We're in a bit of a hurry." Alfred responded.

"I'd be honored to take you both to the command level. As soon as I drop off my current two passengers, I will be right with you- oh would you look at that! They're getting off on your floor, how convenient!" the elevator sung out.

Alfred shoved Marcie to one side of the elevator door while he leaned up against the other. He gave her a quick nod which she returned. The light atop the elevator flashed once more and the A.I. proclaimed loudly, "Welcome to floor three, enjoy your stay!"

The door slid open and out walked two guards. Alfred slammed his elbow down hard on top of the closest one's head, and the man fell to the floor with a groan. Beside him with lightning speed Marcie had sliced the other guard's neck with a blade drawn from the end of her armor. Alfred looked at her, surprised by her lack of mercy.

She looked up at him, nonchalantly adding, "What? I'm an assassin, remember?"

"Fair enough. Hey elevator you don't have video capability, do you?" Alfred asked nervously.

"I'm afraid I'm far past the need for video cameras, I locate passengers by their heat signatures. Ooo it must be a bit toasty on the Iron Pinnacle today, my last two passengers appear to be taking a nap on the cold floor there beside you!"

"Right yeah, a nap. To the command level!" Alfred ordered, and him and Marcie stepped inside the doors as they closed behind them.

The elevator buzzed in excitement as it began to climb up the levels of the warship.

"So what's the plan once we find Sham-Bon?" Marcie whispered to Alfred in a hushed tone.

"How thrilling! The two of you are here to thank the royal king for saving the planet, aren't you?"

"Wow, you are so much smarter than your cousin- yes as a matter of fact we are! Could you tell us where his office is?" Alfred asked innocently.

"I'd be delighted! When you step out my doors you'll see a large glass wall- there's a door in the center that will take you to his Highness' office. It also happens to lead out onto a deck, for a marvelous view of the sky!"

Marcie and Alfred exchanged a determined look-now they knew where he was. The elevator wished them well as it opened its doors and let them out on the command level of the warship. In front of them a little ways there was a large glass wall, so clear that it was almost impossible to tell there was anything between them and the office at all. In front of the doors there stood just one man, wearing a bright neon pink tuxedo with sunglasses covering his eyes.

"It's one of those neon guys from the roller-rink! What should we do?" Alfred whispered urgently over his shoulder to Marcie.

"I don't remember any of the men in the roller-rink wearing pink. Trust me, I killed more of them than you. Let me handle this, you just try to get through the gate while I distract him." she replied as the man approached.

"Who are you two? Why are you on the command level of the ship? This floor has restricted access. Now back on the elevator- both of you. Hey! Where are you going?" the man turned and yelled to Alfred who had slowly been creeping around him toward the glass doors.

"Uh I'm uh-" Alfred stuttered.

"He's looking for a bathroom, it's an emergency. We're friends of the royal family and have been staying on board as guests of His Lordship. Say, don't I know you? Your name wouldn't happen to be Pink, would it?" Alfred watched as Marcie acted out her little show.

"Hey yeah, that's crazy! My name *is* Pink, how did you know?" the man looked dumbfounded and the hostility had left his eyes.

"Oh, I'd recognize that handsome face anywhere. And that dashing tuxedo- my I fall so easily for men with a sense of fashion."

Alfred could have erupted in laughter from the astounded look on Pink's face, but instead he said, "Hey Pink, so you think you could let me use the can or not. Cause things might be getting messy in this hallway soon and I wouldn't want you to be the poor sucker mopping up another guy's piss, you know what I mean?"

Pink turned and looked at Al with disgust as he replied coarsely, "The lavatory is down the hall over there, third door to your left." he turned back to Marcie who smiled.

"What was that about handsome and stylish you were saying?" Pink smiled dumbly back.

While Marcie continued to distract him, Alfred had now reached the glass door. He tried to open it but it must have been locked from the inside. Alfred couldn't see anyone on the other side so he pulled his Rift Blade from his belt and made a small circular cut into the glass near the handle. A purplish cloud had filled in where he had cut into the glass, and slowly he reached his hand into the portal and pulled the door open by the inside handle. He pulled his arm back through and the portal closed, but he managed to catch the door before it landed back in its place and walked silently inside the office. The rule of the rifts didn't apply as long as some portion of his body remained on the original side.

It certainly appeared to be an office fit for a king. There were ornate leather sofas and armchairs in the center of the room. They sat on an enormous rug which had the Huck Family crest sewn into it. The walls on either side could hardly be seen at all, with the lustrously polished wooden book shelves that surrounded them. On the far side of the room there was a grand desk that was adorned with gold accents. The chair behind the desk was empty, but Alfred walked out past it to see a well-dressed man standing on a large open balcony overlooking the sky and ground beneath the warship. The man turned around, holding a mixed drink in his hand. Alfred's muscles tensed when he saw it was the face of Sham-Bon.

13 ABOARD THE IRON PINNACLE

Marcie was starting to grow tired of pretending to listen to Pink talk about how important he was to Sham-Bon and the Huck Family. A million thoughts raced around her mind as she stood with Pink's arm around her, feigning interest in some story he was telling. She needed to get to Alfred and help him kill that conniving bastard before Bratvia got demolished. She doubted that Aaron and the villagers would be able to hold off an army of that size for long, especially the royal military. They had a tank and a giant warship and hundreds of men. Bratvia had a couple dozen villagers armed with arrows and spears. Marcie's attention snapped back to the present as Pink asked rudely,

"Are you even listening to me? Hey you! And where's your friend, he's been in the bathroom an awful long time. Wait a minute. Your armor looks kind of- aaargh...ugh." Pink was interrupted by Marcie's blade piercing into his chest, where she then jerked it hard to the right.

Pulling her arm and the blade back out she made as if to run toward the glass doors but something grabbed her leg.

"Wow, you're fiesty! That was a nice shot, but it's going to take a lot more than some special armor to kill me." Pink spoke from the ground, his tuxedo was covered in blood and cut down the middle. Marcie's eyes opened wide as she noticed the wound she inflicted had sealed itself back up.

Thinking quickly, she tried to shake Pink's grip off her leg, but he was incredibly strong. Much stronger than even Ardmon, she thought. Raising both her arms she slung them down quickly at Pink who was still on the floor. Four throwing stars stuck into him, pinning him down by his arms and legs. He gasped in pain and released Marcie's leg. She stepped away from him quickly and glared down at him with a look of triumph.

"Now, maybe you can answer a few of my questions since it seems you're a bit pinned down at the moment. First off- why do your wounds heal so quickly?"

"Because I'm not a delicate human, like you. The king has blessed his most loyal servants with the ultimate gift- *immortality*." he sneered the last word as if in spite that Marcie wouldn't be able to kill him.

"You mean you can't die? And Sham-Bon- he can't be killed either? Surely you can't be invincible?" Marcie questioned the man in disbelief.

"As if I'm going to give away how you can kill my leader, let alone myself. What do you take me for? To tell you the truth I don't even know how one *could* kill an immortal! Surely you'd have to be a god or something."

"Damn it Alfred, you're going to get yourself killed and it's all my fault for dragging you into this." Marcie spoke to herself.

"What's that? The little bathroom boy is in on this too? Well, he must not care much for you if he left you here with me while he goes running off to his death. Anyway, I believe I've had quite my share of lying around for the day!" Pink howled in pain as he pushed himself up, forcing the throwing stars to rip through the tendons in both his arms and legs.

The wounds began to seal themselves up rapidly now that the tissue was no longer being blocked by the metal stars. He lunged with stunning speed at Marcie, who wasn't expecting him to be able to attack while his skin was still regenerating. She managed to sidestep to the left and duck, pushing upwards with all her force and sending Pink flying over her shoulder.

"Hey, not bad." he praised. "You're pretty quick. Too bad you're not immortal, I wouldn't mind spending an eternity with you. What do you say you give this whole rebellion thing up, and I'll have Sham-Bon perform the procedure. Man it's a crazy ride, but if you survive it- the power is out of this world!" the man laughed maniacally and smiled, exposing two rows of bright white teeth.

"I'd never join the likes of the Huck Family. They've brought nothing but endless suffering to my people and this entire planet."

"If that truly is Altarian Rue Armor that you wield, then I suppose that makes you a liar. You must be Marcie- yes there's no doubt about it. And you certainly have joined the likes of this family before, why you've done more than that girl! You were raised in it. Little Marcie *Huck*- my haven't you grown up!"

"Shut your mouth. My last name isn't Huck- it's Devlash, and yes it's true Sham-Bon took me in as a child and trained me but he is *nothing* to me. Once I learned the type of man he was I only stayed to plot against him and steal Gosia's Crystal to save Hemphion myself."

"Foolish girl. I suppose you would have been quite young when it all happened. Your last name might as well be Huck, for that *is* the name of the man who saved your pitiful existence. I was there, oh yes, I remember the day well. It was the task that earned me my immortality. Poisoning two Bratvian villagers, parents of a little girl only a few years old."

Marcie was starting to freak out, how could this man have killed her parents? Her memory was fuzzy, but she remembered her parents growing very sick with disease and dying in the sanctuary when she was just eight years old.

"That can't be true, my parents died of the disease from Hemphion's- no, wait the sun…" Marcie's eyes clouded up and she fought back tears as Pink picked up where she left off.

"The sun was never going to explode, that's right. Put it all together now, come on. You must be a smart girl if Sham-Bon raised you."

Marcie glared back at Pink with a newfound hatred.

"He never raised me- I saw him less times than I can count on one hand throughout my childhood. He paid for everything though- the best instructors, combat trainers, swordsmen. But now I'll use it all against him. I see that he must have had you force my parents to get sick. But why?"

"Why to make the whole thing even more believable, of course! Your parents were the very first ones we introduced the disease to in Bratvia. And what do you know, it spread like wildfire over the years. Sham-Bon had the disease developed to kill off everyone middle-aged or older throughout the villages and compounds across Hemphion. By doing so, he has now gained the faith of all Hemphion's youth. Not only for saving the planet, but for putting an end to the so called sun disease that killed off all their loved ones."

Marcie was done talking. She couldn't believe her parents had been used as poison apples to kill of the others in her village. There must have been so many others that had perished in the rural villages all across the planet. It makes sense, she thought, that the city people and Parliament would have been more likely to evacuate sooner when news of an epidemic *and* an exploding sun reached them.

"You shouldn't have told me you killed my parents!" Marcie screamed as she slid out two long red metal blades from each of her arms.

Pink looked at her in surprise as she slashed into his side and arm, sending a gush of blood out onto the glass wall behind him. The look of agony faded quickly from his face and he reached his hand into his side, pulling Marcie's blade out and lifting her up by her arm.

"I told you that hurts. And you can't kill me- so enough *already*!" he swung and threw her by the arm, sending Marcie crashing through the glass wall.

***

"Al Moreno, I must admit it is so wonderful to see you again. You are too kind to have gone through all this trouble to bring me my crystal." the man flashed a sinister smile as he spoke in a snobbish tone to the Rift Resolver.

Alfred studied him, taking in everything he despised about the man that stood before him. His unnaturally black beard that should have been gray for a man his age. His face that showed no wrinkles and the only sign of aging was that his hair was speckled with grey. He was tall and slender, and carried with him an aura of confidence. He no longer wore the black tuxedo he had on in Jenni's Roller-Rink. Instead he wore jet black pants that carried into an expensive looking pair of golden boots, likely the sacrifice of a rare animal's hide. Around his exposed chest there was a black silk robe, truly fit for a king and covered in intricate patterns. On top of his head there sat a crown, shimmering with a gold that rivaled Gosia's Crystal.

"I won't let you get away with all this. You're a monster Sham-Bon. A phony. The little prince who had to wait until he was far beyond his years to take the throne. What, did you kill daddy to speed up the process too?" Alfred taunted the king.

"Evil as you may see me to be, no I was not responsible for my father's death. He was a good man who simply lacked the ambition necessary to put an end to the mockery of our family. He played his meaningless part in the parades and ceremonies and whatnot- but never did he seek to restore the power that the Huck Family has forever been entitled to on this planet."

"You went about it all wrong Sham-Bon." Alfred began. The king raised his eyes with interest as he took a drink from his glass.

"Do go on, tell me how *I* could have done better. It's not as if *I'm* moments away from demolishing this village. And then who will they listen to, *you*? They'll believe an outsider over their king who has saved them all from death?"

"You spent your life waiting to take over. Somewhere along the line you likely wasted countless years chasing immortality- just so that you could keep your ambition alive. And yet, had you campaigned through the people and won their trust fairly as your father had- you could've brought back more genuine influence to the royal family. But you were greedy, you wanted it by any means possible. It didn't matter if that meant killing the people you wanted so badly to rule over, or sending them away scared for their lives from the planet they've always called home. You *disgust* me."

Sham-Bon sat his drink on the balcony railing saying, "I couldn't very well have left it to chance with the odds of all that political nonsense working out being slim to none. The plan I devised took years, and it is because of that planning that my family's name is about to return to its rightful legacy. Now I think I'll put an end to you, before you try doing something stupid."

The next few moments seemed to go by in slow-motion. Alfred turned to look behind him as something crashed through the glass wall. There was someone lying on the floor- it was Marcie! He saw Pink walking menacingly towards her.

"Marcie, are you al-" Alfred's cry was cut short as Sham-Bon attacked him quickly with his back turned, stabbing a longsword that gleamed with a red hue through his chest so that it stuck out the other side.

"ALFRED NO!" Marcie's scream echoed around the king's office.

Sham-Bon flashed his sinister smile and wickedly announced, "Welcome home my child."

14 ON THE FRONT LINES

Aaron Flux thoroughly enjoyed being a Rift Resolver. It was an independent job where most of the time the Resolvers would be sent on solo missions. Never before had he been in anything close to an all-out war, and he had certainly never been in charge of leading the rebellion against a royal military's forces. But despite all this, he believed in Al Moreno. Flux had joined the Society a year before Alfred turned eighteen and was eligible to sign up. Even so, Moreno had been able to surpass him in all of his training and even received his Rift Blade a year before Flux got his. Alfred had escaped from gods, taken his rift mission far beyond the call of duty, and risked his own life countless times for the safety of a planet he knew almost nothing about. If Al could do all that, Aaron thought, the least I can do is buy him some time.

The battle wasn't looking good for the village of Bratvia. They had managed to hold off the first squadron of soldiers until now, shooting at them from behind the cover of the North wall. Flux ducked down for a moment, catching his breath and trying to think of a plan of action. He watched in horror as a villager beside him fell with a thud to the ground. Flux crawled over to him, careful to keep his head out of gunsight.

"Hey, hey! Where are you hit, talk to me man!" Flux was searching frantically for the entry wound, but the man could say nothing and only made an eerie gurgling noise as if something was bubbling up in his throat.

Flux noticed the man had his hand clasped tightly against the side of his neck.

"No, damn it!" Flux yelled as the man's hand fell limp and the light left his eyes.

Another villager crawled quickly to his side shouting, "Sir we've got to move. Now! They're clearing way for the tank."

Flux glanced at the dead villager beside him once more, his heart filled with guilt and sorrow. Then he remembered he had a duty and turned to the others around him.

"Everyone get back! Off the wall now, they're gonna blast it down! Push back to the sanctuary, we have to defend it!" he yelled to anyone left that could take heed of his directions.

The remaining dozen or so men leaped and crawled to the rope ladders. Flux made sure they had all gotten down safely and then followed after them swiftly. He ran after the group of villagers racing for the sanctuary's doors on the opposite side of the compound. The man who had warned him about the tank was running just ahead of him and Aaron forced his legs to pick up the pace to catch up to him.

"Any news of Lornan?" he asked in between catching his breath.

"No sign of him yet."

Aaron shook his head. He had sent one of them, a man named Lornan, to try to get help from the closest village. It was a larger compound called Granderfall in the Eastern section of the forest. The man had taken Ardmon's motorbike and the roundtrip could be made in a few hours, but there was no telling if he had been able to avoid the Huck men on his way.

"You guys must have some sort of radio or something we can use to contact the other village, don't you?" Flux asked hopefully as they arrived in front of the sanctuary along with the other men.

"I'm afraid it's no good sir. Ardmon has been trying to reach Granderfall all morning and it seems that the airship is sending out something that blocks our radio signals."

"Damn it, can I have nothing?" Aaron said angrily to himself.

The men had spread out around the front side of the building forming a blockade. The doors to the courtyard opened quickly and Ardmon ran out before they shut back behind him. He ran up to Flux and was about to say something but all voices were lost in the sound of a massive explosion. Aaron looked to the North wall and saw a massive chunk had been crumbled to bits by the tank's round. Huck men were already beginning to climb over the rubble, breaching the compound.

"Ardmon, get all the men inside the sanctuary. Have them climb on the wall of the courtyard and get all the civilians in the main lobby. We need the higher ground. Give them hell."

Ardmon nodded and went to gather the villagers, leading them through the gates into the courtyard. When the last one had safely made it through Ardmon called out to Aaron, who was still outside of the building.

"Hurry, come on! They're getting close!"

"I'm staying here. I'll take out as many as I can and I'll fall back to cover when I need it. Do not open those doors, no matter what!" Flux demanded.

Ardmon looked as if he were about to argue but the Huck army was now in full view. Soldiers filled the main road as far back as the eye could see, and more were still coming in through the wreckage of the wall. The sturdy man dipped his head to Flux and disappeared into the courtyard, the gates closing firmly behind him.

Alright, Aaron thought, now's my time to do something. Flux stood alone in the center of the road. The remainder of the fighting villagers had climbed onto the walls around the courtyard and sat on top of them- aiming down with whatever weapons they had left.

Flux dropped flat to the ground, momentarily out of view of the oncoming men. Hurriedly, he reached for his Rift Blade and took a strange looking gun from his side holster. It had every component of a normal handgun, only instead of a barrel there was a holding contraption on top. Flux took his blade and set it in the gun, tightening the sides of the contraption until it held the Rift Blade steady in place. He pulled the trigger in ever so slightly and the tip of the blade began to glow bright purple. He released the trigger and stood up.

"Over here, *fuckers*!" he screamed his own personal version of a war cry.

The Huck men who were closest to Flux were now made fully aware of his presence. Seeing this, he began to run away from the sanctuary, ducking quickly behind a plasti-crete building as bullets hit the dirt where he had been standing moments before.

"Hey, there's one over there! He must be crazy or something telling us where he's at. These stupid savages." one of the men who had seen Aaron yelled to the others.

Most of the men in the first squadron were now running in the direction of Flux. Aaron stepped out into a second road between the buildings, while further up ahead several dozen men ran towards him. The first row lifted their guns, firing round after round of energy ammunition directly at the Rift Resolver. Flux was quicker though, pulling the trigger of his Rift Blade gun all the way in now- sending out a blast of purple beam which swallowed up all the bullets that headed for him. The beam continued to travel out toward the first dozen or so men that had shot. Aaron aimed the gun from side to side, forcing the ray of rift portal to cover up a larger area. It sucked up every last trace of the men and their weapons.

One of the Huck men who had been fortunate enough not to be in the line of Aaron's shot called out to the others in a panicked voice, "Go back to the main road, he's got some kind of death-ray!"

"Death-ray, yeah you wish buddy. I'm sending you guys all to a creepy island full of possessed Russian nesting dolls. Waaaay out on the edge of the galaxy."

Flux laughed to himself as began to run after where the men had headed back to the main road.

It looked like there was now a great deal of confusion going on amongst the royal military. The second squadron had started to enter the battlefield. However, the men in the first group were now running into them in an attempt to get away from Flux. The Rift Resolver paused for a moment behind the cover of a building. Combining so much of himself with the Divine Energy was beginning to take a toll on his stamina. He wouldn't be able to do that big of an attack again for a while. Aaron looked around the corner and saw that the men of the village had begun raining arrows and energy bullets at the enemy. Taking advantage of their confusion, he pulled the trigger in once quickly and shot a rift into the middle of the street and then another smaller one directly in front of him. Pulling a regular gun from his right-side holster he fired all the rounds in his first clip into the smaller portal. Then he took off running behind the larger one in the street. The men who saw him had no chance to shoot for they were now receiving Flux's gunfire that emerged from the portal in the road.

Aaron tried to make for the door but was met by another group of Huck men cutting off his path. The villagers were too tied up to notice he was trying to get back into the cover of the sanctuary. He knew he didn't have enough energy to muster an attack on the men. So Flux did the only thing he could think to do- he shot himself in the chest with his Rift Blade gun.

Aaron had only ever experienced being shot by that particular gun one time before. It was when his personal mentor in the Society had first given him the weapon. The man had invented the contraption himself and had decided to pass it on to Flux when he graduated from training. His mentor had shot him once and teleported him across the room, making sure he knew the pain the gun inflicted when it transported its target. Aaron once again felt that gut-wrenching pain, right in the middle of his chest. He got to his feet slowly and found himself inside the walls of the courtyard.

"Ugh...remind me to aim for the foot next time." he groaned as he climbed up the front wall and found himself beside Ardmon.

"You don't. Look so. Good." huffed the man.

"Speak for yourself there wheezer. Need to lay off the cigarettes, eh?"

"I'll never smoke another if we make it out of this alive, hell- maybe a cigar instead!"

"You got a deal there." Flux replied in agreement.

Just then, a chunk of the wall they hunkered below blew to pieces, taking a hit from an energy round.

Ardmon jumped back down into the courtyard followed by Flux.

"That was a close one." Ardmon commented.

"Let's just be glad they haven't managed to get that tank in here yet." Aaron shot back.

The two men made as if to head up the other side-wall but were stopped by a shouting boy with a bow. It was Jashi.

"Lornan...Granderfall..." the boy was completely out of breath and could hardly be understood in between his gasps for air.

"What? What are you saying- what's happened to Lornan?"

"No...they're coming...haven't stopped running-met Lornan leading a group of villagers here. Shouldn't be much longer...South Gate." as the boy finished he collapsed to the ground, passed out from exhaustion.

"This kid's going to be a hero when this is all over with. Take him into the main lobby and get him checked out by Mother Via. When those men reach the South Gate, lead them back around the side of the compound and try to get behind those bastards. And watch out for that tank!" Flux directed.

Ardmon nodded and scooped Jashi up in his arms, carrying him quickly toward the lobby's doors. Flux headed up the wall that the front gates were set in and climbed onto the ledge. He peeked his head up over the wall and blasted a beam of rift portal on the men who had tried to intercept him as they were firing rounds into the doors. The Huck men disappeared in screams of pain and agony. Aaron ducked back down quickly as he heard bullets whizz past him.

"Alright Moreno...I've bought you some more time. Now hurry up already!" he yelled out, raising back over the ledge and firing both his guns into the never-ending streams of the Huck military.

15 OVER THE EDGE

Alfred's body began to convulse, and he forcefully coughed up mouthfuls of warm blood that seeped from his mouth onto the cool white floor below. He fell to his knees as his attacker slid the sword back out of his chest. Alfred looked at Marcie who was desperately scrambling to her feet in an attempt to help him.

"No... Marcie, stay back." Alfred managed to choke out as he pushed his arm down onto the floor, using it as leverage to get back on his feet.

She ignored him, reaching him quickly and helping him to stand.

"How interesting, I must say I wasn't expecting this. I'd love to hear how my Altarian Rue Longsword hasn't killed you, Rift Resolver. That was a fatal blow for the average man."

"Well," Al began to explain, "maybe that's because I'm not average. And hell, maybe I'm not even a man. I really don't even know or care anymore- but I *am* going to kick your ass."

Henry lit up from inside Alfred's pocket and said hesitantly, "Sir, you probably could have phrased that differently…"

Pink had now walked up and stood a little ways behind Marcie and Alfred. He laughed at the A.I.'s comment before saying to his boss, "Can I kill these two yet?"

"Kill the girl, she is a traitor afterall. I'll take care of Mr. Moreno here." the king ordered his guard.

"Alfred what do you mean? You're not human?" Marcie looked at him, startled.

"No time now, can you handle that guy? Henry, help her out as much as you can." Alfred grabbed the egg out of his pocket and set it on the floor.

Pink was now rushing at Marcie from behind, but Henry had lowered out two sets of small tires- turning himself into a mini egg-shaped tank rolling speedily around the floor. He flashed his high beam golden lights into the eyes of his friend's attacker, causing him to miss Marcie and crash head-first into a nearby bookshelf.

Marcie shot a vein-chaser into Sham-Bon, who had once again lunged at Alfred with his sword. It distracted the king for a moment. Even if it couldn't kill him, it was still tearing through his skin causing extreme pain and messing with his aim.

"Me and Henry can handle Pink. Alfred I'm so sorry."

"Don't be. I'd do anything for you. Now it looks like that giant highlighter is getting back up- tear him apart!" Alfred exclaimed ardently.

They held one another's gaze for a moment longer, a glance that could only be understood by two individuals who had fallen in love. Then Marcie ran back toward Pink who had regained his bearings, followed by Henry zigzagging all over the ground behind her.

Alfred's attention was instantly refocused on Sham-Bon, who was ripping the vein-chaser out of his chest as it neared his heart.

"What's the point in ripping it out? I never took you for one to have much of a heart." Alfred gibed.

"Seems like yours can take quite a piercing." Sham-Bon spat back, seeing the wound he had inflicted in Alfred's chest had sealed itself back up.

Alfred swung a right-handed punch at the king's face, but Sham-Bon dipped to the side at the last moment causing Al to slide past him and run into the balcony railing. The king wasted no time and leaped onto him, forcing him hard to the ground. Something shiny fell out of the Rift Resolver's jacket pocket and went skidding across the floor. It was the Crystal of Gosia.

Sham-Bon made the mistake of glancing at the crystal and in that split-second Alfred grabbed his Rift Blade and sunk it deep into the king's side. But something strange happened. Sham-Bon released his grip from pinning Alfred down and fell beside him, clutching where the blade had struck him, obviously in pain. Alfred got to his feet while Sham-Bon struggled to do the same. When they had both gotten up the king removed his hand- behind it a gaping hole had appeared, showing through his body and out the other side.

"What have you done to me?" he asked furiously.

"Well I gotta say, I tried to send your entire body into the ultimate abyss but it seems as if only a part of you has gone."

"Ultimate...abyss. What is this you speak of?" Sham-Bon was trying to stall as he steadily became more use to the hole in his body. It must have hurt like hell, but he was regaining his strength bit by bit.

"The Place of No Return, as the Rift Society calls it. A portion of your soul has been completely destroyed- it is in a place of utter nothingness. For this reason, it is a tactic only used by Rift Resolvers on the foulest scum in the Universe. An honor I've bestowed upon you." Alfred took a mocking bow.

Sham-Bon looked as if he were about to ask more but Al charged at him now, wielding his Rift Blade in his right hand.

"I know you're buying time old man, but I thought I'd at least let you know where your soul will be lost to for all of eternity." Al spoke through gritted teeth, his blade meeting the king's sword.

***

Meanwhile, Marcie had her hands full dealing with Pink. She didn't dare try to catch a glimpse of how Alfred was holding up, but she could hear the sound of his Rift Blade hitting against Sham-Bon's Altarian Rue sword. Damn I want that sword, she thought, while dodging one of Pink's punches- kicking out with her shielded foot and landing a kick in his groin.

"Ow! Damn, I may be immortal but take it easy on the sensitive spots will ya?" the man complained.

Marcie said nothing and continued her assault, sending an onslaught of throwing stars into the man. He was on the defensive, and dove to the side to avoid the stars, only one sticking into his leg. But Marcie knew she had only needed one to stick. Yes- she was on him now. In the swift moment while he was distracted in an attempt to pull the star out of his leg, she sliced through his outstretched arm. It fell beside him, amputated. Pink managed to land a blind kick on Marcie that sent her flying back. She got to her feet to see him standing- but his arm hadn't regenerated as she suspected- the wound had merely sealed itself so he wouldn't bleed out and die.

"You won't have a very fun eternity if I cut all your limbs off." she called out.

"I'm really starting to not like you, bitch." he said nastily.

"Watch your language, that is a woman you're speaking to!" Henry scolded, blinding the man with yet another beam of light.

Marcie's emerald eyes sparkled with an enraged fire, and she lunged at Pink with extraordinary speed. She fell on top of him, knocking the man hard onto the ground. But Pink had managed to stop her, twisting his legs around her torso and trapping her in place.

"Not so tough are you now, little Huck girl." he sneered.

"Oh me? Says the one cut in half!" she yelled.

Pink looked down in confusion and saw that Marcie's armored knee had slid out a medium-length blade, which she rammed into his abdomen.

He let out a cry of pain as Marcie kicked her knee forward with all her power, forcing the blade to slice through Pink's stomach all the way up to his neck.

The man writhed around on the ground as Marcie stood up, relinquishing the blade back into its place within her armor. She watched, slightly disgusted, as Pink's body attempted to string his skin and organs back together. The flesh on either side of his cut stomach reached out as if to connect, but seemed unable to span the distance. Marcie approached the man, sliding a blade out of her right arm.

"Here, let me save you the trouble. Bitch." she said as she swung down with her arm, slicing Pink's head clean off.

"You're a true gentleman, Henry. This guy could use some pointers." she said to the little A.I. as she picked Pink up by the hair on his head.

His sliced neck had sealed itself back up in a gruesome looking stump. Henry and Marcie hurried back towards the viewing deck with Pink's head swinging in her right hand as she ran. As they made it onto the balcony they found Alfred and Sham-Bon locked in an intense duel.

"Alfred!" she yelled.

Alfred's eyes remained only on Sham-Bon, but he yelled back as they continued to exchange blows with one another.

"Marcie! Look you've got to get-" Alfred paused for a moment as he ducked under the king's high-swinging blade. "You've gotta help Flux and the others, they can't be in good shape."

"But I can't leave you here alone!" she yelled back.

"Leave this to me, Marcie. Go help the others."

"I won't leave you!" she called back defiantly.

"I'm probably going to regret this move in the long run." Alfred said bluntly to Sham-Bon, whose face turned into a look of confusion.

Alfred swung at the king, who managed to move his sword in time to block it. But Alfred punched upward hard with his left fist. Sham-Bon stumbled back for a moment and Alfred did something very unexpected. Something he would indeed likely come to regret. He threw his Rift Blade at Marcie, and her face lit up in shock as it stuck into the hand holding Pink's head. The head fell to the floor and Marcie disappeared into a rift portal.

Alfred sprinted over quickly to where his blade lay on the floor beside Henry and the severed head. Sham-Bon made a run at him, but tripped over his feet as Henry blinded him yet again.

The man rubbed his eyes roughly and turned back to see Alfred standing, now re-armed with his weapon.

"How cruel of you Moreno. We're more alike than I thought. To kill a girl who so obviously loves you, just to keep her out of your way? Why we're practically twins, my boy!"

"I didn't kill her. I sent her safely back to the main lobby in the sanctuary with a minor hand injury. Seriously though man, you managed to convince an entire planet that its sun was exploding and you honestly think I just murdered the girl I love?"

"Oh, my! A little romance story playing out right before my eyes! I've never really been much into the chick flicks."

"Sir, you love Marcy?!" Henry asked excitedly, completely ignoring the dire situation at hand.

"Did I say l-love...jeez. Well now's not the time for me to be sorting out feelings, okay Henry?" Alfred stuttered back.

"You know, you should be asking for my blessing. I'm the closest thing she's ever had to a father, after all. Always did have a soft spot for the kids, especially when you have their parents murdered slowly by disease. But what do you know- they all turn into betraying brats." Sham-Bon raved.

"You are nothing to her. You've killed so many, ruined so many other's lives. Making an entire planet believe their home would be destroyed. There are no words to describe a soul like yours Sham-Bon. I pray to the Universe that you are truly one-of-a-kind because men like you don't deserve life. That's why I'm sending you to the eternal emptiness."

"Oh what's that, eternal emptiness you say? As appealing as that sounds I think I'll have to pass on the offer. Aren't you forgetting about something Alfred, I told you it was far too kind of you to bring me the crystal." Sham-Bon opened his palm, in it glimmered the Crystal of Gosia.

Alfred looked surprised to see that the king had picked up the crystal, but then again he had lost track of where it was during the intensity of their battle.

"Oh would you look at that! Is that shock I see on the great Al Moreno's face? You do realize this gives me the power of the god Gosia himself!" Sham-Bon roared as he took his sword and cut a slit into each one of his palms.

Alfred watched, puzzled, as the man clasped his hands together with the crystal between them and yelled, "GOSIA I DEMAND YOU GRANT ME YOUR POWER!"

The king tensed his muscles tightly as if preparing to endure some sort of extreme pain of the god lending him its power. He stopped a moment later and looked at his hands in bewilderment.

"Why...why hasn't it worked?" he mumbled.

"You guys are all so uneducated about ancient Universal artifacts. The crystal's a gateway to Gosia's realm, and the only way I've been able to use it is with my Rift Blade- which you don't have. Oh, and a ceremony with a bunch of creepy old men under the moonlight. Looks like you shouldn't ever have gone chasing after the crystal, eh little prince?"

"I am a *KING!*" Sham-Bon spoke indignantly. "So what, I wanted to use the crystal to conquer other planets eventually- but at the end of the day being emperor of Hemphion can keep me content for awhile until I find a new way." The king threw the crystal brutally at the floor, and it skidded into the far back corner of his office.

Alfred ran at the man, managing to stab another gaping hole in his chest. Sham-Bon fell back in pain, but wiped one of his palms across Alfred's face.

"Eww, come on man! Blood to the eyes, really?" he wiped his eyes frantically in disgust against his already bloodstained jacket.

It didn't do much good and Alfred found his eyes twitching with irritation as he had to dodge Sham-Bon's attacks. The man's reflexes were definitely slower than before, but even so Alfred struggled to avoid them through his watering eyes. He found himself getting pushed back farther and farther across the balcony. Sham-Bon swung down viciously with his longsword and Alfred leaned back- the blade's tip grazing across his chest. He tried to regain his balance but the king kicked him in the stomach, sending him flying backwards.

Alfred found himself falling over the railing and he reached out his hands desperately to grab anything that could give him a hold. His left hand found nothing but emptiness, but he had managed to clutch the rail with his right hand. He felt his muscles tense as the weight of his hanging body fought against him.

"Henry, the crystal! Get the crystal!" he shouted to the egg who was scooting around the floor in sheer panic.

"Yes sir, hang on sir!" he voiced back with worry as he scurried into the main office.

Sham-Bon, feeling the effects of two pieces of his soul being utterly destroyed, limped over toward Alfred who was fighting to pull himself back to safety. He was having a hard time reaching up to the ledge to grip it with his other hand. Finally he had grasped it but had to release it immediately as the king swung the Altarian Rue sword down onto the ledge where his hand had been moments before. Alfred reached as if to grab his Rift Blade and teleport himself to safety, but had to jump his gripping hand over on the railing again as Sham-Bon swung down with his sword.

"You're not teleporting out of this one. Tell me, how does it feel to see everything you care about crumbling away right in front of you? And here you are, their last hope- hanging on to dear life!" the king laughed crazily, the hatred for Alfred shimmering in his eyes.

Sham-Bon swung down once again, and Al barely managed to jump his hand over and avoid his sword. He felt his grip starting to slip with the fatigue of shifting his body weight around to dodge the attacks.

"Why do you bother? We both know you can't keep this up much longer." the king stated grimly, and Alfred knew he was right.

Henry had picked up the crystal with an extended claw, and held it tight out in front of him as he zoomed back towards the balcony. He was about halfway across when he heard his companion yell.

"Henry, I need the crystal NOW!"

Henry processed the level of urgency in his friend's voice instantly. Not a nano-second later he had arrived at the only possible thing he could do in that moment to give the man who had given him life, a chance to live himself. Henry may not have had a soul, but in that instant he ignored the calculation of Alfred's survival probability (0.000041%) and he felt a new sensation. One that no A.I. had ever experienced before. It was faith.

The little golden egg reached its claw back far and swung it forward, catapulting Gosia's Crystal into the air at a very specific trajectory. In the moments that Henry watched the crystal rotate through the air, he had time to explore over 3,000 thoughts. But he chose just two:

1. The percentage for Alfred's chance of living ended in the numbers 041- the name of the elevator that had taken him to his date on board the Lonely Hearts Neptune Cruise Ship.

2. The Universe has a sense of humor.

Alfred tried to swing himself over to avoid Sham-Bon's sword, but it had been too much for his body to manage any longer. He felt his hand miss the railing and he began to fall through the air. In the first few moments of his plummet he stared at the triumphant face of Sham-Bon who gazed down at him. Al decided he wouldn't spend his last moments looking at the face of the bastard who had killed him. He made as if to close his eyes and accept his fate, as he felt the air rushing all around him. Then a raging thought surged inside of him.

I have always accepted the destiny that the Universe has long set out for us all. I have served my whole life to protect it from those who attempt to disrupt its all-knowing flow. So Universe, he thought in his head, if you don't want it to end like this, and I can do anything at all to prevent it, please give me a damn sign!

Alfred opened his eyes, a glimmer in the air immediately catching his eye. It was Gosia's Crystal falling just above him.

"Henry you're the best! *UOGH!*" Alfred choked as the crystal fell into his mouth and down his throat just as he had opened it to thank his friend.

Alfred could feel the crystal lodged in his airpath and forced himself to gulp down hard so that he could once again breathe. He felt it slide down his throat as he swallowed. Not exactly what I had in mind, he thought to himself.

Suddenly it seemed as if he weren't falling as fast. In fact, everything had happened quite quickly and he was surprised to see he was only a dozen or so meters from the ledge he had tumbled over. He looked to his right and almost pissed himself as he saw a giant owl diving through the air beside him.

"Duplication, Al Moreno." it said softly to him, and its voice reached Alfred clearly, as if the words had been put directly in his mind.

The owl disappeared. Alfred once again felt time shift back to normal and he found himself plummeting seemingly a hundred times faster.

"Gardtrof!" Alfred's shout was lost in the blasting wind around him.

Alfred closed his eyes once more, paying no attention to his impending impact on the ground far below the warship. He cleared his mind and focused his energy until he could feel its presence pulsating throughout his body. He thought of the crystal- now inside him. If he was going to try to become one with the crystal's energy, it being inside him didn't seem like such a bad thing. Alfred ignored the Universe's Divine Energy that he had so long been trained to accept and harness with his own. He blocked it out entirely until his mind was clear of everything but the powerful spirit that seemed to be resonating out of the crystal in his stomach.

Alfred felt the crystal's energy combine with his own, until the overwhelming sensation of its power seemed to vibrate through every nerve in his body. He focused for the first time on not one location to teleport his body to- but three separate places. Alfred's eyes snapped open.

16 MULTIPLE MORENOS

The Rift Resolver found himself back on the balcony of the command office. He felt strange, almost as if he suddenly weighed no more than the air that surrounded him. He looked up to see Sham-Bon kneeling on the ground and inspecting Pink's severed head. Further ahead of the kneeling king he saw something incredibly bizarre. It was him, standing just a little way in front of the shattered glass wall of the office.

Alfred's awareness suddenly flashed into his body across from Sham-Bon. The man was talking to the head and hadn't yet noticed his arrival. I need to be in both places at once, he thought, I'd say it's impossible but I don't think I believe in that term anymore. He focused on where his body stood near the balcony railing. Slowly, yes, he felt it! He raised an arm up gently and each copy of him raised it simultaneously. Then he moved his left arm on one copy while moving his right on the other. Yes, he was getting the hang of it- he was able to be in both places at once and have each body perform its own separate functions.

"What the hell! How are you alive, how are you here?!" Sham-Bon roared, noticing the Alfred that stood in front of him.

Pink's head spoke from where it sat on the ground beside the king, "Hey, I thought you said you killed that guy?" he asked ignorantly.

"I did kill him, it's impossible!" he declared.

There should be one more, Alfred thought, feeling for the presence of the third copy he had tried to split himself into. Yes- he felt it. There it was in the main lobby of the sanctuary. Take control, yes you can do this, he encouraged himself. It felt as if he had grown even lighter, but he had done it. His soul was split into three individual copies of his body, and he had command of them all.

"Nothing is impossible, you should know that Sham-Bon. Even you claim to be immortal. Your soul may remain forever, but it'll spend those countless eons in the ultimate abyss."

Alfred ran at Sham-Bon with his Rift Blade, using both the body that stood in front of him and the one the king was unaware of on the balcony behind him. Sham-Bon managed to meet the front copy's blade with his own.

"I suppose I'll just have to kill you yet again. Perhaps you'll be more of a challenge this time around." he ridiculed.

"This match's outcome has already been decided. And I'm sorry to tell ya Princy, but I win." Alfred flashed back as he forced his blade harder into the longsword, knocking it from the king's grip onto the floor.

The second copy of Alfred had now reached Sham-Bon, and he wrapped his arms around the unsuspecting man tightly so that for all his strength he was held still. The king forced his head to angle behind him, his face dumbfounded when he saw another Al Moreno was his captor. The front copy of Alfred wasted no time and thrust his Rift Blade in and out of the man's body several times, careful to avoid his copy's arms. The second copy released his hold as Sham-Bon fell to the floor screaming at the pain of his soul being sent into the eternal emptiness, piece by piece. He had only the strength left to glare at the Rift Resolver in pure hatred as Al sliced upward through what remained of his patchy body. The king's eyes flashed once more with despise as what was left of him vanished into a dark void, forever trapped in the Place of No Return.

Alfred stood up from where he had kneeled on top of the king's body. He looked over to his second copy and they reached out to connect a high-five.

"Now that's what I'm talking about!" they said at the same time.

"Hey over here! You can't leave me here, please!" Pink's head shouted from the floor.

"I think I know what to do with him." Alfred's second copy said.

"Be my guest." the other Alfred replied.

The copy picked up the head by its hair and ran a few yards before tossing it into the air and punting it off the balcony with a hard kick. Pink yelled something inaudible as his head disappeared over the side of the railing. The copy took a bow and Alfred allowed that portion of his soul to return to him.

"Henry buddy, I don't know where you're at but I hope you're okay." Alfred spoke aloud and he allowed the current portion of his soul to connect with the one he had summoned back down in the village of Bratvia.

***

Alfred found his third and now only copy opening its eyes to the sound of someone yelling.

"Wake up! Alfred, please don't be dead...please." it was Marcie crying beside him.

"Not quite." he said sitting up and taking hold of the girl whose eyes became filled with pure relief.

Alfred held her embrace for a moment longer before he let go and got to his feet, giving her a hand up.

"Look, no time to explain really. I'm about to do something really, really crazy. It's going to sound like a terribly stupid idea, but you have to trust me. You haven't seen Henry around here have you?"

"I trust you, and no I haven't seen him since you threw a knife into my hand! Now, what's this plan of yours?" Marcie asked accusingly.

"Right, sorry about all that. Yes the plan- so I'm going to run out into the battle now, armed with only my Rift Blade, and hope it all works out the way it's looking in my head right now." Alfred stated plainly.

"No, Alfred! That's the worst plan I've ever heard!" Marcie yelled at him.

"You said you trusted me, no take-backs!" he yelled and then quickly sliced the tip of one of his fingers with his blade, sending him outside the sanctuary onto the main road.

"I really know how to pick 'em." Marcie said to herself as she got to her feet and ran out to the main gate.

She climbed swiftly over the courtyard wall and opened her eyes wide at the sight before her. There were dozens upon dozens of Alfreds running through the streets of the village. They each moved according to their own will and slashed through the lines of Huck men. When a copy got hit it simply faded and a new Alfred sprung up in its place- charging right back into the thick of the battle. Marcie shook her head and ran up the road with her vein-chasers ready. Might as well give him a hand, she thought, as she sent the chasers into two of the men closest to her.

Meanwhile, the much more sufficiently armed forces of the Granderfall village had managed to sneak around and launch an ambush on the backside of the royal military. They had even taken down the tank using a mobile energy-artillery unit. The men of the other village were blocking the royal military in on one side and the army of Al Morenos kept them at a standstill on the other.

The military men were running around in sheer mayhem trying to escape. A few made it over the village walls but most of the Huck men had been trapped in the middle. The fighting came to a sudden halt as a voice echoed throughout the village speakers.

"Hellooo there, men of the Royal Huck Military! This is the new captain of the Iron Pinnacle warship. Your leader has been killed. Surrender now if you don't want me to blast these energy cannons down on you. You can ask a friend of mine- my aim and timing are impeccable!"

"Henry!" Alfred yelled out from one of his copies. "Man I missed that voice!"

He wasn't sure if the A.I. had been able to hear him but it looked as if the message had worked. The remaining soldiers lowered their weapons to the ground and placed their hands behind their heads. Alfred allowed the many spread out pieces of his soul to once more come together into a single body. The Rift Resolver felt relieved to feel the empty sensation fade from him, but he bent over out of breath. He looked up from his gasping to the sound of two familiar voices.

"A little out of shape? Well, doing whatever the hell you just did will probably leave you feeling a little winded I suppose." Aaron Flux's voice rang out as he ran up to support Alfred, who was finding it hard to stand.

"I guess your plan wasn't so bad afterall." Marcie had now reached them and supported Al from the other side.

"I think I can manage one more rift, if you'll help me do the honors Flux?" Alfred replied, grinning as they helped him walk up to the circle of kneeling Huck men.

"Creepy possessed-doll island?" Aaron asked, raising an eyebrow.

"Man you always pick that place! Then again, I suppose these guys could use a tropical getaway."

Aaron laughed and left Marcie to help Al as he began to drag his Rift Blade through the dirt road in a large circle around the men. Flux removed his blade from his special gun and started connecting the portal until they met on the other side.

"So long boys, send us a postcard!" Ardmon called cheerfully from where he stood nearby the leader of the Granderfall village.

Al and Aaron looked at each other once more and connected the last segment of line in the circle. The men disappeared in a flash, as the circle illuminated in a great purple light that absorbed their bodies. Marcie helped Alfred to walk over to where Ardmon was standing.

"I don't have the right words to express my gratitude to you and your men." Alfred said to the leader of the Granderfall forces, a man by the name of Trugban.

"You should thank Lornan. I must say I found it hard to believe the Rift Society had become mixed up in the affairs of our little backwater planet. But he *did* manage to convince us that the royal family was launching an attack on the village. I suppose you can fill me in on the details of this conspiracy later this evening, Ardmon? We'll need to get the story straight and make the people that are left on this planet aware of what's going to happen moving forward." Trugban turned to the large man beside him.

"Of course, there will be much to do in the coming days. In the coming years, really- it will take a long time to rebuild what's left of Hemphion and get it back in order under a new government." Ardmon replied seriously.

"I'm afraid politics aren't really my thing; you guys will have to sort out that mess on your own." Alfred added with a laugh.

"Come on, you need to lay down. Let's get you back to Mother Via in the Sanctuary." Marcie said softly to him.

"Yeah, laying down. That sounds pretty damn good. And some food, that'd be nice too."

"Perfect, I think Jashi went out hunting again last night." she replied sarcastically as she helped lead him back to the sanctuary.

"Can't a guy just get a nice cheeseburger?" he laughed back.

Most of the Granderfall men began to head back to their village, while a select few remained in Bratvia with Trugban for the next few days to discuss what Hemphion's future held in store.

Flux made as if to follow his friends into the sanctuary, but something shiny in the sky caught his attention. It looked like an oddly-shaped golden rock that was being propelled by something spinning on top of it. Aaron ducked quickly as it swooped at him and landed gently in the front pocket of Alfred's jacket.

"Henry, you're back! How'd you know I managed to survive and kill Sham-Bon? Amazing- taking control of the warship too!" Al greeted his companion who flashed brilliant gold lights in delight as he spoke.

"I didn't know Alfred. I believed."

Alfred said nothing more but smiled as the group continued to make their way up the road to the sanctuary's gates.

17 DUTY CALLS

Marcie awoke early on the morning three days after the battle in Bratvia had gone down. She looked out her bedroom window of the sanctuary to see Alfred chatting with a man of the village in the courtyard. Lornan, she thought, he must be thanking him for managing to bring Granderfall's forces in time to help us. She smiled warmly as she saw Jashi playing with a group of the village children. Henry scooted around on the ground as they chased after him. Her eyes flicked to the doorway of the room as a voice sounded, grabbing her attention.

"So what's next for you Ms. Devlash?" it was Mother Via.

"Our village. It's going to need a lot of rebuilding. And all the villages and compounds across the planet, there's so much work to be done."

"Foolish girl. You've spent your entire life protecting this planet, and you've succeeded, no doubt! But come now, you are young and it sounds as if Trugban and Ardmon have devised a rough plan to get this planet back in the right direction. There's a whole Universe out there for you to explore, and quite a handsome young man to do it with."

Marcie looked at her in surprise, "You really think I should go? But Jashi...and so many are still sick from disease…"

"Jashi will be just fine, he's got me and the rest of this village to help raise him and the other orphaned children. And if some day he wishes to travel off into the galaxy, I will tell him the same as I'm telling you now- go." Mother Via explained gently.

"Thank you Mother." Marcie spoke softly, thankful that the woman had been able to calm her guilty thoughts of leaving Hemphion to fend for itself.

"As for the disease, I believe we have some visitors who have brought remarkable news on the topic. Come into the main lobby- I'll fetch the others."

Marcie was curious, but said nothing and walked out of her room and down a short hall until she came to the main lobby and took a seat on one of the couches. Aaron gave her a wave from the chair he sat in, picking at some animal Jashi had caught and cooked the other day with disinterest. A few minutes later Alfred came in with Henry in his pocket, followed by Jashi and two old men wearing brightly colored purple robes. The last one hobbled in slowly after Mother Via, he was hunched over a wooden cane.

"Marcie, Aaron- this is Barnin and Wardriff- two members of the Gazers." Mother Via introduced the men.

They shook hands politely and respectfully before everyone took their seats. Barnin looked slightly embarrassed as he began to speak, talking to Alfred who sat across from him.

"I must apologize Mr. Moreno, I had long lost my way and forgotten what it meant to be a Gazer. But you, you have restored my faith and for that I am eternally grateful to you."

"I understand, there's no need to apologize. Now why is it you two have come here, you say you bring good news?"

"Oh yes, wonderful news! Extraordinary news!" Wardriff now spoke up in his scratchy voice. "We have regained contact with Hashish and learned that our god never meant to abandon us- why our god is the sun of Hemphion itself- and sacrificed his entire following just to keep us all alive! What's more, he has told us the sun of Hemphion now shines with a new brightness, one with rays that shall cure any of the diseased by radiating down brilliantly upon the victim. He said it was the least he could do as the god of his people, when someone like Al Moreno has done so much."

Suddenly Ardmon burst through the lobby doors proclaiming loudly, "I'm sorry to interrupt, but it's gone! I woke up this morning and went out on the porch for my morning coffee, and I felt the strangest thing. It was as if I was filled with a warmness and then what do I know- the rash on my neck was gone!"

"Well, it appears Hashish keeps his word." Alfred said, tensing in slight pain as he was swallowed up in a massive hug from the man.

"So Ardmon, I hear you and Trugban have some sort of idea worked out on how to get word to the rest of the villages?" Marcie asked as Ardmon released Alfred, sitting down beside Mother Via and Jashi.

"That's right, and it's all thanks to that little A.I. over there! When the four of you leave tomorrow,

Henry says he'll be able to broadcast the message across the planet from on board the ship as it leaves Hemphion's atmosphere."

"The four of you? Who else is going with the Rift Resolvers and Henry?" Jashi now spoke up.

"I'm afraid that's me little man." Marcie got to her feet and hugged the boy whose eyes started to stream tears down his face.

"No. I won't cry." the boy wiped his eyes against his shirt sleeve with a sniffle before speaking again. "I want to grow up and become a great warrior like you, and I'll train as long as it takes and protect this village like you did."

"Oh Jashi." Marcie looked at the boy with soft eyes. "You're already almost as good as me. You'll end up being the best if you keep it up. I'll miss you so dearly."

She held him for a moment longer before returning to sit beside Alfred. The others tried to look away and distract themselves from the heartbreaking scene that had played out in front of them.

"Well Moreno, duty calls. I received a message via a radio transmission that was sent to Henry from the Rift Society. How they know where we are- I don't have a clue! But that's the Society for you, all-knowing and whatnot. Anyway, we've got orders to head to the planet Jared, out in sector nine. We'll receive our next mission there- it's about a three hour flight on a decent starship."

"Why don't you guys just open a rift? Wouldn't it be much quicker?" Jashi, who appeared to have calmed down, asked.

"That's the thing- we can't open rifts to somewhere we've never been before. Well, Alfred here probably can until the crystal passes through his digestive system- but we don't know exactly how all that works and don't want to risk using it if we don't have to."

"So that means you guys have both been to the creepy doll island you sent all those Huck soldiers too?" the boy asked excitedly.

Alfred exchanged a humored look with Flux before saying, "That's right, it was me and Flux's first assignment together. And let me just tell you- that's one place I'm never going back to."

"You got that right! All those Russian nesting dolls hopping out of each other really gave me the heebie-jeebies." Aaron commented and gave a little shiver as if the goose-bumps were returning to him now just thinking about it.

Everyone laughed as Aaron and Al told the story of their adventure on the strange island. The day drifted by peacefully and numerous villagers came to the sanctuary in high spirits- discovering they had been magically cured of their disease when they first stepped outside into the morning sunshine. As the sun made its way slowly through the sky, night began to fall and Hemphion's sun set in the horizon.

"So you're sure you want to come with me? You can still back out now. I know I can be a bit of a handful." Alfred said to Marcie who sat next to him, alone together in the courtyard under the light of Lax and Luts shining brightly above.

"You're my handful Al Moreno." she looked at him lovingly before her voice grew harsher saying, "Besides, I still have to beat your ass for throwing a knife in my hand!"

"Oh it just grazed your palm!" Alfred said back, his voice was filled with humor but his eyes remained fixed intently on the pair of emerald green ones beside him.

He leaned in slowly, putting his hands on her waist, that for the first time in a long time wasn't covered by armor.

She looked back at him whispering softly, "I love you." and her lips finally connected with the man who had truly done everything for her.

"I love you, Marcie Devlash." he whispered back, their lips forced to separate only for a moment as they both smiled.

***

The Rift Resolvers, Henry, and Marcie had taken off from the Granderfall compound in their spacecruiser early the next morning after they had said their goodbyes. Flux spun around in his chair, flipping through a magazine. Marcie sat nearby, currently concentrating on a game of chess with Henry, who moved the pieces with his egg's extended claw.

Alfred walked back into the room, returning from the lavatory.

"Any luck?" Flux asked with a chuckle.

Alfred pulled a small clear plastic bag from his pants pocket. Within it the Crystal of Gosia glimmered brightly.

"Ew!" Marcie exclaimed, seeing the bag.

"I ran it through the sanitizing machine like four times! What else was I supposed to do?" Alfred defended.

"You're sleeping next to Flux tonight." Marcie shot him a comedic look as she spoke.

"Looks like Tea-Bot really did the trick, eh?" Flux questioned, eyeing the small white kitchen robot that stood beside him.

"Yeah, ran right through me! Besides, who doesn't like Tea-Bot tea? Now if you'll excuse me, I've got a crystal to deliver."

"Don't you think Gosia's going to be a little angry with you after all this? Especially after what just happened to his crystal in that bathroom?" Henry asked as he moved his rook forward on the chess board. "Check-mate!" he added to Marcie.

"You're right, maybe I'll bring a peace offering. Tea-Bot, if you will?" Alfred asked, sitting down at an empty table.

The little white robot shuffled over to stand next to where Alfred sat. It poured out a steaming hot cup of green tea as the Rift Resolver emptied the crystal out onto the table, careful not to touch it. Alfred removed his blade from his belt and raised it in the air with one hand.

"Be back in a jiffy!" he called to the others, taking the steaming cup of tea in his other hand.

Alfred slammed the Rift Blade down into the center of Gosia's Crystal, hearing only Tea-Bot's words as he once more entered the colorful tunnel that served as a gateway to the god's realm.

"Enjoy."

ABOUT THE AUTHOR

Mason J. Schneider was born in the city of Des Moines, Iowa. However, his family moved around a bit and he was raised in a small town in Ohio. Here he has had the odd summer job and also worked as a cashier in the local grocery store. He lives there to this day with his cats SneeSnaw and KinKoo. (Yes, they have very strange names.)

Mason's imagination led to him writing *The Wizard of the Night*, a children's fantasy series, and his young adult (he emphasizes adult for this series) sci-fi *Al Moreno Rift Resolver*. He plans to continue to write adventurous tales for as long as he can.

In his spare time Mason enjoys hiking, reading, writing poems, watching movies, and having good times with friends. Growing up his father built a library inside their house, so there was never a shortage of books and this is likely where his love for reading began. In the future Mason hopes to be able to use his writing to help others around the world.

Oh, and he also paid someone to write most of this author bio. Because while he might be confident in his book-writing abilities, he admits he is quite lackluster when it comes to talking about himself. And also finds it really weird referring to himself in third person.

Website - www.masonjschneider.com

Twitter - @mayso35

41936046R00114